Praise for the novels of
Barbara Dickinson

<u>A Rebellious House</u>

"*A Rebellious House* is a delight, and I hope it's the beginning of a series that will match Jan Karon's Mitford Tales."

—Jerry Bledsoe, author of *The Angel Doll* and *Bitter Blood*

"I'm so happy to see the fruits of Barbara's work. She has planted and now we are all reaping. Hooray for *A Rebellious House*. Truth is always a good thing.

—Nikki Giovanni, poet

"Dickinson writes with charm and sparkle...She gives us Old Age Pensioners who have knowledge, dignity, humor, and wit. You want them (and Wynfield) to really exist."

—Ruth Moses, *Greensboro News and Record*

<u>Small House, Large World</u>

"*Small House, Large World* is a charming vignette of a story...a light-hearted tale..."

—*Roanoke Times*

"Dickinson has written more than a novel...In *Small House, Large World*...[the author] again makes the statement that we are never too old to enjoy life's pleasures...a life-affirming view that is worth repeating."

—*Winston-Salem Journal*

<u>*Lifeguards...and Safeguards*</u>

"I have long been amazed that there have been so few novels set in retirement communities...Now comes *Lifeguards...and Safeguards*...If you enjoy Jan Karon, you will enjoy this deftly-plotted, gentle, romantic, and suspenseful novel."

—Lee Smith, author of *The Lost Girls*

"Barbara Dickinson has written a suspenseful, gripping story of Rick and Rose...through this twisted tale of mayhem and mystery. You will be surprised and amazed at the turns of this author's storytelling."

—Adriana Trigiani, author of *Big Stone Gap*

"*Lifeguards...and Safeguards* is smart and touching...and Barbara Dickinson's writing is on the mark from start to finish. Simply put, this is a splendid read..."

—Martin Clark, author of *The Many Aspects of Mobile Home Living*

"Who would have guessed that life at a retirement home could be so lively? Rose McNess...is a lady of the first order, and Barbara Dickinson's Wynfield Farms is enough to make one long for old age."

—Carrie Brown, author of *Lamb in Love* and *The House on Belle Isle*

"I have read both of Barbara Dickinson's books and loved them...I am a senior citizen and...I can only hope that there is a Wynfield Farms and a Rose McNess in my future. These books let you know that it's a privilege to grow old and that every day is a gift..."

—Janet Mears

Also by Barbara Dickinson

Grandfather Jumper and the Cookie Eating Monster
Secrets from My Kitchen
A Rebellious House
Small House, Large World

LIFEGUARDS...
and
SAFEGUARDS

Barbara Dickinson

Barbara Dickinson

Harlan Publishing Company
Greensboro, North Carolina USA

HARLAN
PUBLISHING

Lifeguards...and Safeguards is a work of fiction. Any references to real people, events, establishments, organizations, or locales are intended only to give the fiction a sense of reality and authenticity. Other names, characters, places, and incidents portrayed herein are either the product of the author's imagination or are used fictionally.

Published by Harlan Publishing Company
5710-K High Point Road #280
Greensboro, North Carolina 27407

Book and cover design by Jeff Pate
Cover art and interior drawings by Barbara Dickinson

First Edition

ISBN: 0-9747278-0-6

Library of Congress Control Number: 2003115802

For Hilary,
with joy on her wedding day and ever after.

~~~

It is impossible to name all the people who have inspired, cajoled, and prodded this story into being. There are, however, some that must be singled out for their expertise and wisdom. I thank you from the bottom of my heart.

My deep gratitude to Father James at St. John's; Charlie Bray; Lynn Eckman; the ladies at Townside Gardens; my own breakfast club at CURVES; B.J.; Carol; Tim, Chris and Anne; Jana Janku and Marketa Rogers; Tinnell's and their special ham biscuits; and of course, Hilary Rogers for planting the seed of this novel and encouraging me when the gray cells failed.

Words of thanks are inadequate when it comes to the contributions of my friend, typist and editor, Nancy McDaniel: she is the best, and also Lynette H. Hampton, my encouraging long-distance editor who helped guide me to a smoother landing. As for my husband, I cannot thank him enough.

Also a sincere thanks to my readers who have pushed me to write one more episode about Rose and her friends. I hope that this story "cossets you like a tea cozy" and gives you the same warm and secure feeling that Rose enjoys at Wynfield Farms.

Barbara Dickinson

Sometimes we lock moments deep in our hearts…and years later those same moments tiptoe back to haunt us.

—Rose McNess

No one ever said life was going to be a picnic. Life is what you make of the leftovers after the picnic.

—Rick Conklin

Wynfield Farms and its residents exist, alas, only in the heart and mind of the author.

(Wynfield Farms as described in the informational brochure)
WYNFIELD FARMS—since 1872

Wynfield Farms is located in the Shenandoah Valley of Virginia between the cities of Roanoke and Lexington. The mansion, built in 1872 by railroad magnate Samuel Thomas Wynfield, replicates St. Edmund Hall, Oxford University, where Mr. Wynfield, an ardent Anglophile, received his Doctorate in Humanities. Three generations of Wynfields have enjoyed the house and its surrounding 450 acres of formal gardens, natural woodlands and lakes. The Nottingham Corporation purchased Wynfield Farms six years ago for the purpose of redefining retirement living, and major modifications were made at that time. All of the expansion has been completed with respect for the previous owners and consideration for the future residents' needs.

Wynfield Farms is committed to providing programs of highest priority and superb security for older citizens. This full-service community includes a chapel, bank, library, recreation areas (a nine hole golf course is within the grounds), greenhouse, bus service and managed health care facilities. Living units are available in studio and one or two bedroom apartments, each with kitchenette and spacious storage.

Wynfield Farms' Dining Room, painstakingly restored to its 19th century grandeur, has bird's eye maple flooring, said to have been hewn from trees felled on the grounds. The room also boasts a mantel designed by Mr. Wynfield and carved to his specifications from Carrara marble. Present day cuisine caters to the discerning palate.

Wynfield Farms—where the emphasis is always on individual freedom and comfort and the lifestyle is synonymous with good taste and elegance. The gracious ambiance of Mr. Samuel T. Wynfield's original estate endures.

Wynfield Farms—the perfect place to reside and retire.

S.O.S. for Senior Lifeguards

SPECIAL TO THE ROANOKE TIMES

MARCH 10, 2003—In an unusual and urgent plea, two of Virginia's largest beach resorts have sent out S.O.S.'s for lifeguards to serve during the coming summer months. Both the Chambers of Commerce for Colonial and Virginia Beaches have issued a joint press release announcing they would welcome the services of former lifeguards from the 1950s and 1960s for the 2003 season.

Citing competition from high-tech firms, the managers of both resorts spoke of being "desperate for reliable help." H. Tyler Renman, General Manager of Virginia Beach Shore Activities Division, said "We are at a near-crisis in our employment situation.

Tourist season begins in four weeks and we cannot find qualified help. Having a mature senior citizen manning a lifeguard station is preferable to closing the beach for lack of assistance. The absence of lifeguards threatens not only our economy but also the well-being of all visitors. I know there are former lifeguards out there who are still physically fit and who would welcome a summer in the sun. I just hope they answer our plea."

Mr. Renman and Mr. Wilson Naylor of Colonial Beach request that interested parties write for interviews by March 31 in care of P. O. Box 9997, Roanoke TIMES, Roanoke, Virginia, or e-mail lfgdnow@htdt.com, or call (621) 555-9898.

1

Detroit

The man is neither young nor old, tall nor short, but the length of his legs and bulk of his shoulders suggest that he is no stranger to hard labor. He lounges against the granite column, left foot propped behind him, right shoulder anchoring his upper body. Ducking his head, he leans away from the wind and repeatedly taps the rolled-up newspaper against his thighs in an attempt to generate warmth in his limbs. A fine mist is falling and he brushes the freezing particles from the dark shank of hair falling over his eyes.

His glance sweeps across the deserted expanse of library steps. No one is seeking refuge in the library this evening. A gray and ghostly pantomime of nameless, faceless people jostles by on the city sidewalk adjoining the vast steps. It had snowed two days earlier and Detroit's streets and walks remained slushy and tarnished with the detritus of slow melt off. Workers shuffling by singly occasionally in pairs, were silent, their pace quickened by the evening chill and the mist that had changed into serious sleet. They scurried like so many small animals, drawn instinctively, irresistibly to the one safe place they knew: home.

The man watches this tableau and feels oddly comforted. He's no different from the pack he sees milling by on the sidewalk. Home is what he seeks too, and isn't that what he's just been promised? He loosens the folded newspaper in his hand and smoothes it over his jeans to the creased section highlighted in green marker. The afternoon light has paled from violet glow to dishwater scum and it is impossible to read the small print. Everything blurs; there are no sharp and definable edges even in the black blocks of the headlines. Is it the light or his vision playing tricks on him? He folds the paper and crams it into the pocket of his faded windbreaker. He pushes up the sleeve on his right wrist and searches the scarred face of his watch. No use. If the headlines are invisible the numerals are hopeless. He's been outside for more than an hour. Time to check again with the young librarian at the main desk. She's waiting for him, clearly annoyed.

"There you are. I'm ready to leave and I didn't know what to do with your information," she says.

"You found something already?" He is polite, eager, as friendly as a puppy and full of himself. "Gosh, you're quick Miss Lipscomb. Sorry I'm late gettin' back. Thought I'd use the time to whip over to the police station and see if they had any other means of trackin' my sister. Guess I was gone longer than I thought. All wet, too. And wouldn't ya know, I hit a dead end with the P.D. You say you had some luck?"

"Not luck. Hard work and common sense. You could have done this yourself. Just a matter of punching the right keys on the computer. Here it is." She hands the man a 3" by 5" index card. "I've got to run."

"Hey, wait a sec. Don't rush off. Could I buy you a coffee or something? To thank you for your trouble? I really..."

"No trouble. I've got to run. I'm meeting someone in five minutes. 'Bye."

"Say, thanks for taking time and..." His words sweep out the door with the cold blast of wind that ushered the pretty librarian into the evening.

The man hesitates a moment before deciding on a seat. He sees a vacancy in the corner where a reading light casts a cone of brightness on an empty table. Feeling warmer already, he slides onto the hard library chair. He pulls the newspaper from his pocket and spreads it meticulously, rubbing his thumbs over the folds as if he would like to stretch the column from three inches to six. Only then does he look at the index card that Miss Lipscomb handed him.

"Virginia," he whistles. "This here is my ticket home. And home is where I'll find you, Rose Mason."

He rereads the highlighted article. His stomach growls, reminding him that his last meal was breakfast and that was over nine hours ago. Where should he go for a meal? The Mission over on 9th? Salvation Army? The diner? Yeah, why not the diner? A small celebration in honor of the occasion. He'd tell the old moose-faced owner that he was going where there was real food. Real Southern cooking. Yeah, it was a celebration. He was on his way home. He'd hit the road tomorrow. No more meals at the Mission for a long time.

Wynfield

Broken hip; curse of the elderly, passport to purgatory. Statistics show more people over sixty-five... Rose McNess shakes her head in despair.

Oh. Bother! I wasn't reciting statistics or one-liners when I fell and landed on my backside. More than likely yelled 'Damn' or even 'Damnation.' That's how I feel now, damn mad at myself for being clumsy enough to fall.

Rose tries to find a comfortable position on her narrow hospital bed. 6:30 A.M. At least I can see the clock on the opposite wall. That's the only convenience here, as far as I can tell. I must be getting better; nothing suits me this morning—not the bed, not this chalk-white room, not this old, tired body.

Crash! Boom! Whirr—whirr—whirr!

Rose blinks, shifts slightly to her left, and wonders what she is hearing. A bad dream? Is she still sleeping and in the midst of a nightmare? Crashing thuds, whining high-pitched noises are an inferno for the elderly. Maybe a broken hip *is* purgatory.

Rose stretches to push the call button, when the door suddenly bursts open and a smiling gnome with a mass of unruly black hair jiggles in. The nurse bears a tray laden with a thermometer, assorted medications and a carafe of fresh water.

"Mornin', Miz McNess! How're you doing today? You're looking good, I can say that."

"Good morning back at you, Chickie. I'm just fair this morning. I warn you, I'm cranky. Or at least I *was* until fifteen minutes ago. Can you *please* tell me what is going on outside?"

"The cottages. You must've missed the announcement."

"What announcement?"

"The one about startin' the construction. Twelve new cottages are going up. They're beginning 'em today. Been at it since six."

"I forgot they were to start this soon. But I heard sounds of a chain saw; bulldozers don't make that noise. Even I know that, Chickie."

"Right you are, Miz McNess. That's the old peach orchard. Had one big fir that had to go first, now the little trees. Got a right big crew over there. Probably bring in the 'dozers this afternoon to push all the little ones down. Right sad, ain't it? Old man Wynfield probably planted every one of them peach trees himself."

"I'm sure he did, Chickie. I forgot the cottages were to border the old peach orchard. Guess I didn't realize how many trees were going to be affected. Was there talk of saving any of the younger trees?"

Rose realizes the futility of her question. Here in Assisted Living there would be few to care or even worry about the surrounding grounds. The residents who came here were tired in mind and body, or both. They wanted ministering hands and one-on-one attention, not news of the outside world. And since Chickie and the other nurses had little or no contact with other Wynfielders, they could hardly be expected to know what was going on outside their domain.

"No'm, I've not heard much talk about the cottages. Just that today was the starting date. Big ceremony planned for the hole digging I s'pect."

"I expect so. Perhaps I'll be on my walker then, and not so helpless. How long have I been in here, Chickie?"

"They moved you from the hospital to AL the day after your surgery so let's see. Countin' today, you've been with me ten days. Doctor took your staples out yesterday. Feeling tender on that right hip, are you?"

"Ten days! No wonder I forgot about the cottages! Ten days being out of circulation is the same as, well, the same as six months! Especially at my age. Good gracious, Chickie, please take my temperature now. For some reason I'm thirsty and that cool water looks tempting."

"Sure thing, Miz McNess." After finding out she is free of fever and her blood pressure is normal, Rose swallows her medication and drinks two large tumblers of the sweet, pure water. She allows Chickie to help her into the lavatory and then back to bed. The nurse promises to return with a huge Wynfield breakfast and Rose sinks gratefully on her pillows to wait. She smiles as she watches Chickie's round backside exit.

"What would I do without Chickie in this place? This place!" Rose sighs.

"Assisted living! Assisted Termination is more like it. Another day like all the others. I miss my own room and my own bed and my own belongings. First, I'm foolish enough to trip and break my hip, then I consent to a hip replacement. Now I'm captive in a cubicle where I can't get away from the infernal noise. Even worse is realizing that they are destroying years of precious green and growing creations—all in the name of progress. And profit."

Ten days! No wonder I feel old and sick. And vulnerable. The doctor—funny, I can't even remember his name now—said I was going to experience some confusion after the anesthesia. But shouldn't I be returning to normal by now? Or was I this fuzzy before my fall? I can't even remember how I got here. If I start at the beginning and retrace my steps one by one maybe I can collect my wits. Or pick up the pieces of them. Think it through. Yes, that would help me. Isn't that what I always told the children to do—think it through?

I was in the gardens, over by the bridge. Late afternoon because the sun had just dropped behind the pines in the west. I was walking Max. Max! Where is he? Rose gasps. Her heart flip-flops at the thought of losing her beloved pet. Her eyes suddenly brim with tears. Max, oh poor baby. Now I remember; daughter Annie came and collected Max. Rose goes limp with relief. Her upper lip is wet with beads of perspiration and she shivers with anxiety.

Whew! Glad that came back. Anyway, I was walking Max and we were searching for a scrap of yellow that I had spied from the apartment. The daffodil! The first daffodil! I leaned down to firm the ground around it, and the next thing I knew I was flat on the ground, and Max was barking like crazy. And the knot on my head? She touches her forehead gingerly. At least there are no stitches. I must have hit a root or a rock and knocked myself out. How long was I out?

I recall waking up and thinking, Oh no, not my hip. Strange, I knew it was broken. Thank goodness, I had sense enough to lie there like a squashed bug. Then who was it who came? Annie? No, no, it was Romero. Wonderful Romero, man of all works and a true friend since my move to Wynfield. Romero and one of his twins, just out for a late walk. And he said he told the child to sit with me while he ran to call the rescue squad.

Rose sighs. Her head aches thinking about the past ten days. She closes her eyes and blurred images spring into being— speeding ambulances, banging emergency room doors, blinding blue-white lights of operating rooms, the swimming faces of her three children. Why were they always whispering? Whispering like a radio that she was unable to turn off or tune out. Did they really think I was going to die?

Was that it? Was their tough old mother going to be one more geriatric statistic?

And who was my surgeon? Selby? Sellig? No, he's an actor. Sellcor? That's the insurance company. Sellridge? That doesn't sound right either. Sellsoe. That's it! Well, I'm making progress if I can remember *Sellsoe*. What was it he said? That I'd need a new hip anyway if I kept on the way I was going, so why not now? What did he know about the 'way I was going'? Rose frowned. He said my fall was a lucky accident. Sort of in the nick of time, he put it. Ha! Little does he know! He doesn't have to lie here and listen to that pandemonium. Or fight the boredom of four walls. Rose, Rose, how could you be so clumsy?

And poor Max. Rose's thoughts return to her Scottie. Maybe it's a good thing he's with Annie. He'd be terrified of these loud noises. How did Annie hear about my fall? Oh, the new director. Now what's her name? Think Rose, *think*. First name is Paula. Paula. Rhymes with—valentine. Gallentine. Paula Gallentine. Annie said Mrs. Gallentine kept Max in her office until she and Jim picked him up. I must thank her properly when I get out of here. Can't imagine Miss Moss doing that! Mrs. Gallentine has been good for Wynfield Farms, Rose thinks sleepily.

How can I be so sleepy? I feel as if I were floating down a wide river that goes on and on. I might drift forever. But this isn't me! I never get tired and I never nap. Rose allows herself a rare splinter of worry. I don't like the Rose McNess I am becoming. Is this one more wrinkle of old age? Or was my head injury more serious than they've admitted?

Sitting as straight as she dares, she smoothes her short hair. Chickie was right: her wound is tender. "Enough of this pity party, Rose McNess! Exactly one year ago, you led your friends across the British Isles. Now look at you! Where is your spirit? Your energy? Your sense of adventure? Today you *will* master any therapy they throw at you and get back to regular living. Enough hanging of the crepe. One hip is not going to be the end of you. There is simply too much to do!"

Chickie chooses that moment to return, bearing a steaming breakfast tray. "Visitors already?" she asks, eyeing the room expectantly.

"No, no, Chickie, I was scolding myself. Declaring my independence. I'm a pitiful sight laid up in bed like this, taking your valuable time and care. I plan on leaving you soon."

"Not before breakfast, I hope. Cook's done a number on the poached eggs you like. Sound pretty good to you?"

"Wonderful! I'm famished. And I promise to eat every morsel. I'm going to need my strength for Godzilla." The nurse raises a black eyebrow. "Actually, her name is Inge. Privately, she's Godzilla, Godzilla the Great. She's a marvelous therapist and today we tackle the stairs. Up *and* down."

"Got something else for you." She fumbles in the pocket on her broad bosom, extracts a crumpled envelope and hands it to Rose. She digs again and finds a folded piece of pink paper.

"Your nice lady friend asked me to bring this to you straightaway. Just the one letter and this today."

"Must be Ellie Johnson. She's the only person I know who enjoys writing notes. Likes for me to keep up with the news." Rose's curiosity overcomes her hunger and she adjusts her glasses.

"I certainly will be glad when I'm able to use my contacts again, Chickie. These glasses just add to my image of being old."

```
Rose!
We are all missing you! Frances is
threatening to chain herself to the
peach trees. She and Bob Lesley are
in a tizzy! Know you can hear the
racket from A.L. Hope to get down
to see you after lunch, as I know P.
T. wears you out in the morning.
Love and xxxx,
Ellie
```

Rose is aware of Chickie watching her. She glances at the other envelope and sees an Ohio postmark. "Do I know someone in Ohio? Can't be important. I'll save that to read later." She stuffs the envelope into the pocket of her robe.

"Hmmm, Chickie, seems the cottage construction is causing an uproar among the residents of Wynfield Farms."

"They got that right, uproar it is," said Chickie dourly. "Body can't hear herself think."

"Some folks aren't in favor of this new construction. A few have even talked of throwing themselves on the peach trees to prevent them being cut."

"Well now, that's a stupid thing to do. They's old trees for the most part. Not going to bear fruit any more. Haven't been any new trees planted there since old man Wynfield passed. Nope, those trees are good for firewood and that's the all of it. Ever smell peach wood burning, Miz McNess?"

"Can't say that I have, Chickie," replies Rose.

"Smells just like peach jam boilin' on the stove. And that makes mighty good eatin'. I can remember one time skimmin' the foam off a kettle of peach jam, smacking it on a piece of store bought white bread, and crammin' it in my mouth. And then my mam, she about skimmed *me*, that's for sure."

"Chickie, you have just managed to make me forget my fellow residents' misery and arouse my appetite. Let me at those eggs."

They laugh together, and for the first time Rose feels the day might just turn out better than she thought possible. The letter with the Ohio postmark is still forgotten.

Wynfield Farms rejoices that Rose McNess has been released from Assisted Living and is recuperating in her own apartment. Although she calls her recovery "interminably slow," Ms McNess continues to make remarkable progress. What do you bet she is up and about and walking our halls by the time you read this? Rose McNess, all of us have missed your cheerful and graceful presence among us and only wish you the speediest of returns to good health!
Paula Gallentine,
Resident Director

(Until Mrs. McNess returns to her editorial duties at *Wynsong*, *Ms* Mueller and Ms Gallentine shall endeavor to publish the newsletter Ms McNess has single handedly turned into the spirited "Voice of *Wynfield Farms*." We ask for your patience and indulgence as we persevere in shoes that cannot be filled with our pitiful efforts!)

P .G., Resident Director,
K. M., Secretary

(EXCERPT FROM *WYNSONG*, WYNFIELD FARMS' WEEKLY NEWSLETTER)

"Today is the day!" Rose announces to her oft-used and dented tea kettle plus an army of mismatched cups and saucers. She pours herself a cuppa. This morning I face the world. If not, I'll scream if I don't leave these four walls. I left A. L. three weeks ago. I hate for the staff to keep bringing my meals, my mail, my *everything*. Not to mention what my friends are doing. As Tennessee Williams put it so eloquently, I am dependent on "the kindness of strangers".

I wonder if Mrs. Gallentine was shocked when she saw my apartment. It does look rather tattered. She was so kind, really, seeing that my plants were watered, the floors dusted, the rugs vacuumed and linens changed during my absence. Homecoming was far less traumatic because of the work she and Annie did. Almost like returning from a trip. Except the only souvenir I picked up was a new hip.

Rose moves her teacup a little closer and slides forward on the ladder-back chair. She glances towards her living room, sunny with morning light streaming through the tall bay windows. Her eyes sweep over the scene: faded wing chairs, the upholstery an all-over pallid blue instead of the once outrageous pattern only she remembers; end tables and her treasured butler's table littered with books, unread magazines, and family photos. The walls hold three oil landscapes by Virginia artists—Harriet Stokes, Jim Yeatts, Ann Glover—

whom she regards as dear friends and mentors. No matter that every lamp looks chipped, every shade needs dusting or replacing, every pillow on the couch begs to be plumped.

I need Max to give them a good nesting. How I miss that old nuisance! A house is simply not a home without a dog. At least my house isn't.

I'm a sentimental old fool when it comes right down to it. How does Annie describe my apartment to her friends? 'Early Spartan'? That description suits me just fine. I've had a lifetime of dusting and polishing. Downsizing was designed for people like me! High praise, indeed, to be of the 'Early Spartan' school.

Rose sips her tea (now cold) and rests her elbows on the table. Her gaze lingers over the comforting scene she has created.

From Rose there emanates a steady and convivial friendliness that immediately envelops everyone she encounters with warmth and well-being, much as a tea cozy cossets and warms a pot of tea. Rose's home mirrors this same snug sensation of quiet comfort. Visitors invariably remark, "Your home looks just like you!" Rose accepts this identification as a compliment; cozy and familiar.

Well, my tea is cold and time is slipping away. I cannot sit here and daydream all day. I should pluck out a few of those tired flowers in this basket. And I must remember to thank Jocey. She is a wizard. These blossoms look as fresh today as they did a week ago.

Rose grasps her walker and leaves the safety of the kitchen chair.

She makes her way to the living area. Absently flicking the dust from the top of a book, Rose's eyes light on a small, square shadowbox resting on the same table.

Why is this box even out? Oh, Paul's children. They begged to see "granny's medals." 'Rose's memory box' Mother proudly called it. Bless her heart, she was so proud of my winning those six swimming medals that she created my personal trophy case. But my swimming triumphs happened years ago. No one at Winfield is interested in past history. What concerns us is the future! She carries the box to her bedroom and places it high on the closet shelf. She notices her old bathrobe has fallen off its hook onto the floor of the closet.

"Oops, better hang this relic up. Sort of forgotten it since A.L. Annie's spoiled me with my lovely new one. I'm not throwing it out now, but—what's this?"

Rose spies an envelope protruding from the robe's pocket.

"Well, I'll be...Here's the letter that came while I was all laid up. I remember when Chickie brought it in to me. The Ohio postmark—yes, this is it. And I still have no idea who in Ohio could be writing me."

She shuffles over to her bed and tears open the envelope.

```
Dear Rose:

    Looks like I'm in your neighbor-
hood in Virginia this Month and thought
I'd drop by to see you. It would be
swell To See you and go over Those Old
Times!!! I'll write, when I Get to
your part of the world.

    Your friend,

    Rick Conklin
```

"Rick Conklin? Who in the world is Rick Conklin? Certainly doesn't ring a bell with me. 'Old Times'? *Must* be a case of mistaken identity. Well, it's not stopping me today."

Rose checks her appearance in the hall mirror.

Not bad for an old dame. At least I'm not stooped - *yet*. I've probably shrunk an inch or so, but I'm not going to measure. Hope this new hip bone is the same length as the other. I can't afford to be gimpy along with all my other infirmities.

You need a haircut, Rose. Getting shaggy around the edges. And your nose is shiny, but then it is always shiny. And those freckles! Thought they might've faded in the wintertime. How many lemons did I rub across my face as a teenager? Dozens, I know. Whoever started the rumor that lemons fade freckles? Well, not bad, I repeat, for an old dame who can barely remember what day of the week it is.

A parting glance at the floor reveals Max's blue and white dog bowls, pristine and empty, glistening in place. I'll have Annie bring doggie bones when she returns with Max. His treat box is as empty as the hole in my heart.

Rose stops for a moment, poised between the kitchen chair and her front door. Sighing, she thinks about the adventure she is about to begin. Why am I so nervous? I don't look that different. Greeting old friends for the first time in three weeks is not like walking into a room full of strangers. When I moved here everyone *was* a stranger. Now they are all good friends.

And the best part is, we're in this together. Wynfield is a fortress against the winds of fortune, a haven for fragile souls. *And* bones. Probably what Thomas Wynfield had in mind when he designed this home for his wife. He's not the only one who called his home a castle. It's mine, too, and I'm ready to greet my subjects in the Castle's own pub!

All right, world, here comes Rose McNess, springing free at last!

Rose shuffles awkwardly along the corridor leading to *The Rose and the Grape.* She is edging toward the corner when a familiar voice stops her.

"Rose! I can't believe my eyes! How wonderful to see you vertical." Lib Everett, a close friend since Rose's arrival at Wynfield, plants a warm kiss on Rose's cheek. Her scent is delicate. Lilac? Perhaps. It promises spring blossoms and sunshine. Lib Everett, the no-nonsense librarian accustomed to wearing shirtwaist dresses and gum-soled brogans is totally transformed in her role as bride. A surprise marriage to Arthur last year in Oxford had been the talk of that town—

and Wynfield Farms.

"Oh, Lib, how grand to see you. And you're wearing a heavenly scent. One of Arthur's little surprises?"

Blushing, Lib nods, then asks, "This is your first outing, isn't it Rose? Really, you're making remarkable progress. Not that I expected otherwise, mind you."

"I am getting cabin fever in my apartment, Lib. As much as I enjoy my own company *and* my books *and* my computer, I miss people! Isn't that why we all moved here? I long to be with my friends and hear what is going on. I hate not knowing if Bob Lesley is cheating at bridge or if the chef has changed his menus in my absence and if I've missed all the good movies. That is my identity; 'Curious Snoop'. You understand, don't you, Lib?"

"Absolutely," replies her friend. "I don't play bridge so I can't help you there. But Chef Leon wouldn't dare leave, and the movie schedule has been spotty at best. Today, however, you are in luck. The Wynfield Art Show opened yesterday, and I think you'll agree that it is smashing. And I'm so excited; Arthur has already sold one of his paintings."

"Why, that is exciting Lib. Something to crow about. How could the Art Show have slipped my mind? I'm sure I put the dates on my calendar then simply didn't check. Every day seems to run into the other; I can't keep up anymore. But I am thrilled for Arthur. Is there anything he cannot do when he puts his mind to it? Including capturing you?"

Again, it's Lib the blushing bride, "He is something special, isn't he? But do come along and see for yourself. You'll be amazed at the number of *artistes* we have here."

Rose stopped her slow pavane with the walker. "If you don't mind, Lib, I am just not up to it today. One thing at a time, and I was heading for the pub—"

"How thoughtless of me! The Art Show can wait. That would overtax you. We'll go to the pub where you shall have the place of honor."

They resume their stroll, and in a voice both low and restrained, Lib continues, "You know that a few of us enjoy gathering here before lunch for coffee, tea, or the occasional sherry. By this time I guess you'd call us regulars. The Men's Investment Club meets today, but they should be finished, and thirsty. And full of talk. You'll have a chance to greet all your friends at once, Rose. Perhaps I might whisper a few things in your ear before we get there. A word to the wise, so to speak."

Rose stopped instantly, alert as a cat at a mouse hole. The Lib Everett she knows is not given to idle chatter, much less idle gossip.

"Oh?"

"I don't want to alarm you, but you'll notice a big change in Major Featherstone. I call it his war stage. Arthur insists it's flashbacks. Memories of his training and career moves and war experiences are crowding in on his mind. We think that 9/11, the war in Iraq, and all the security threats and everything, have changed him. Particularly since you saw him last."

"A lot of folks have changed since 9/11, Lib. Not to mention since Iraq. But the major? This really concerns me. Noticeable changes? How is his health?"

"Oh, he looks fit. Perhaps thinner, but he is exercising and walking more. He does roll the grounds with Vinnie. But he's snappish, fidgety even peevish. Not the gentle soul we've known in the past."

"Do you think it could be the dreaded A-disease, Lib?"

"I, I...it's too early to tell, Rose. I just don't want to think along those lines."

Rose digests this news and asks, "Anything else, Lib? Other red flags I should watch out for?"

"This one's even more delicate, Rose. But it's your friend Ellie."

"Uh oh. I think I know what's coming. Tippling a bit much, Lib?"

"Just a little. Not all the time. She's so gregarious that she really doesn't need a drop of anything to liven a conversation. Her laugh and grand humor perk up every group.

Once and a while, though, she does go overboard."

Rose nods and smiles in understanding. I can put the lid on that situation. What are friends for, anyway? "Please tell me this is it, Lib. No more, I beg of you!"

Lib looks stricken. "Oh, Rose, I hope I haven't made you dread seeing everyone again. No, nothing else, and when you consider that we are *all* old and peculiar, why, the major and Ellie have no more quirks than the rest of us. Maybe your fresh eyes will see this in a new light. I'll be happy if you prove me wrong."

It is my unpleasant responsibility to report that within the past three weeks small plastic bags of debris have been found in secluded
areas of Wynfield Farms' hallways. One bag con-
tained a large box of used household matches.
That this could be a potential fire hazard speaks
for itself. If a resident has *any* hazardous materials he or she wishes to dispose of, or has any
questions about such materials, please see Ms
Mueller or me. We will be more than happy to
dispose of these items for you.

Paula Gallentine,
Resident Director

(EXCERPT FROM *WYNSONG*)

As Rose pauses on the threshold of *The Rose and the Grape* and contemplates the pleasure of greeting many of her close friends, little does she suspect that a few miles away another old friend is hoping to see her again.

The occupant of Room 14 in Daleville's SuperTen Motel is neither sleepy nor interested in the television program that blares from the corner.

Damn! Nearly twelve. How did I sleep so late? Gotta do some thinking and planning. I've got to see Rose before I head to the beach. What've I got, cash for four, five more days? Sure won't go far if I have to stick around here too much longer. Course this room's not going to break me. What a dump! No wonder it's cut-rate for travelers. Who else would stop here? Rick Conklin lazes over to the television and switches it to OFF. Cheap bastards, not even a remote.

He goes back to the bed, stretches his lanky body on top of the grimy coverlet and folds his arms beneath his head. He begins to formulate his Master Plan. Rick always likes to get the lay of the land before committing himself to anything. What is this Wynfield Farms anyway? Is it legit or a sham? Is it an institution like the place in Iowa where he worked as an orderly? How do the employees dress? Uniforms or regular clothes? What kind of people *live* out here in the sticks? Of course, Rick tells himself, he is not applying for a job. He is just thinking of the place where Rose lives. Retirement community. He guesses they exist in Michigan, but he has never heard of one. Rick laughs aloud at the thought of his old man and old lady in a *retirement community.*

What the hell would my old man be retired from? Beating his wife and kids for twenty years? Pounding sheet metal at that failing factory? Retirement community my ass. Must take money to buy into one of them. Rick chides himself for not asking the librarian to explain such places. It is a foreign phrase in his limited vocabulary.

Okay. I case it first. Can't be far from here and I'll hitch a ride out tomorrow. I'll look it over and learn when to return and surprise Rose. Surprise is going to be my best friend for the first meeting. And then—damn! Didn't I write something about taking her out to eat? In what? With what? What was I thinking? Rick chews the cuticle on his left thumb and frets over his hospitable, but impossible offer.

Then he relaxes and thinks of the happy alternative. Rose will be so pleased to see him she will invite *him* to eat. He could be charming to her friends; he *would* be charming. Were they all as old as she? What sort of a place is this Farm, anyway? Would they be interested in hearing about his summer job? Hey, they might even have a swimming pool at the retirement center. Sure they would, old geezers like to swim. And Rose used to be a swimmer. Wonder if she did much of that any more? They would talk about that. They would talk about the old times, the good times, even the sad times at Virginia Beach.

Immensely pleased with himself for coming up with the beginnings of a plan, Rick Conklin flops over on his side and sleeps as if he has not slept in the last two days.

Rick Conklin, alias Eric Lithgow, alias Eric Monson, alias Richard Crebolt, is programmed to catch a snatch of sleep whenever, wherever he can. As far back as his memory allows he is running, breathlessly running from something. As a child, it was from a drunken and abusive father. In his teens, a pandering carnie. Later there were cheating bosses and demanding women who wanted more, more, more.

His father was the worst. Never content to let his two sons read comics or ride bicycles or play with buddies their age in Dexter, South Dakota, he constantly bullied Rick and Jason. "Clean out the sheds, mow the lawn, shovel the snow, haul wood and pick up the rocks in the back field." When he or Jason didn't move fast enough, off came the old man's belt with the wide, silver buckle that sliced the skin like a razor.

When the carnival came to Dexter that spring, Rick knew his chance had come. Without a note to his mother, brother, and definitely not his father, he slipped into the night as the carnival was beginning to pull away and hitched a ride East with one of the barkers. He had no regrets, even when the seedy barker tried that monkey business with him. Rick wasn't wise enough in the ways of the world to know what the man had in mind, but he sensed it wasn't right. So he moved out, and on. Rick joined the tawdry world of the carnival in the middle of tenth grade.

Rick's schools were the open road and his playgrounds the mean city streets. He observed life as he lived it and buried himself in books whenever he could. He borrowed, bought, and occasionally stole, but he always had a book under his pillow wherever he called it quits for the night. He remembered riding the carnival train through Kansas, using his flashlight to read Hemingway's *The Sun Also Rises*, and thinking that Spain must be a million miles away and Hemingway a genius to make it come alive on paper.

Rick grew and filled out the extra inches until his body was lean and muscular. Hard work landed him decent jobs and he was diligent and a fast study. If a boss got ugly, tried to cheat him, or sounded too much like his father, he walked away. And immediately found a job more to his liking.

Among his knapsack of survival skills, none served

him better than his genuinely sweet smile. He was handsome in an almost unfinished manner, much like a piece of
sculpture that begs for one additional slash from the artist's
chisel. He was blessed with a pair of steel-blue eyes, luxuri-
ant iron brown hair, even teeth and a cleft chin. When seeking work in private homes or restaurants, he always sought
the woman in charge. His good looks and gentle manner never
failed to land him a job.

When Rick turned eighteen, he hit Atlanta. It was early
June. He had never known such heat. Scouting around the
pricey residential area of Buckhead he saw yard after yard
with swimming pools beyond gated fences, gleaming turquoise
jewels set in verdant lawns. The people who owned these
gems needed someone to change the filters, rake off the
morning's debris, and periodically clean the pool bottoms.
All, perhaps, for a few bucks a day and quick swims while
the owners napped. Rick thought he would give this a whirl.
Sure different from the carnival. And light years away from
South Dakota.

He got lucky at the second house. A young mother
with three whining children hired him on the spot, desperate
for someone to watch her kids in the pool while she raced to
a church meeting. Rick didn't bother to tell the woman that
he couldn't swim. But the kids were small, and he could sit
in the shallow water, and watch them, all while staying cool.
He liked the little ones. Mostly, he liked the idea of kids doing the one thing he had never had a chance to do: play.

The young mother bragged to her friends about the
hunk she had just hired. She lined Rick up with four other
jobs. The summer in Atlanta was the best of his life. He
watched older children swim and memorized strokes and
breathing techniques. He had plenty of time to practice, when,
as he had hoped, the smaller ones went in to rest.

By the 1960s, lifeguard jobs were tickets to romance.
This was a time of affluence, Mustang convertibles, cheap
gas, and vacations at the beach. Rick answered an ad in *The
Atlanta Constitution*: "Lifeguards NEEDED Now!" He didn't

care where he worked. To a kid from the prairies of the Midwest, one beach looked the same as any other. When the reply to his inquiry had said he was to report to Virginia Beach, Virginia, he thought: why not? He'd never been in the state of Virginia.

July of 1961 was a scorcher. And the most important month in young Rick Conklin's life. Amid gallons of suntan oil, bronze bodies and screaming children, Rick Conklin fell in love.

Her name was Rose Mason. Rick had just turned twenty; Rose was an Older Woman. She and a girlfriend had driven to Virginia Beach for a long weekend. They called it their "final fling" before starting teaching jobs in Roanoke.

Rose never knew of Rick's feelings for her. Rick had been careful to keep all of his emotions hoarded as securely as his meager possessions in the boarding house on Atlantic Avenue. Traveling as much as he did, Rick was constantly exposed to prying eyes. Personal privacy was his last single treasure. He was close-mouthed, evasive, and silent about his past and his future, except when he met Rose Mason. He wanted to share everything with her.

Not that he had more than the slimmest of chances. He stood aside and played joker to his fellow lifeguard, Reed Chenowski. Reed was okay, and they enjoyed the good-natured teasing of vacationers, especially girls, about being the "Reed and Rick" twins. Having identical initials wasn't their sole similarity. Neither young man had family. Neither had plans for a future beyond the close of the beach season. Reed had attended one year of junior college in Tennessee and had saved a pile of money from his last job in Memphis. He always had plenty of cash, and delighted in courting girls with tall cups of ice-cold cola and hot dogs when he took his lunch break. Rick was more cautious with money. He understood too well that when cool weather came he would hit the road again. Virginia Beach was not a place to hang around in the winter. Rick thought Reed was too full of himself, too slick. Reed's one-year of college made him boastful and cocky.

Reed ingratiated himself with Rose by questioning her about Ayn Rand and philosophers Rick had never heard of. While he was flattering Rose on her brainy answers and complimenting her on her swimming, he was also getting chummy with the girlfriend. Rick had long forgotten the other girl's name but not the horrific events of that one July afternoon.

He knew he had been making progress with Rose, getting her to talk with him between shifts. And good ol' Reed, the girlfriend had the hots for him and he was too polite to cut her off altogether. If he had, Rose would take offense and then Reed wouldn't stand a chance with *her*. Rick bided his time, talking to Rose a little more each day.

She was the prettiest girl he had ever seen: small boned, with an oval face and short blondish hair that sort of curled up around her forehead. And clear blue eyes. Or were they blue-green? He wasn't sure. She had a handful of freckles across her nose and cheekbones, just light freckles, as if they had been sifted on there. But what had made Rick's heart leap when he saw Rose and her friend saunter down the beach that first day was not physical beauty. Oh, hell no, there were dozens of girls with better figures, bigger bosoms, bigger butts, all strutting in front of the lifeguard stands hoping for a pick-up. There was an indefinable air about Rose Mason. It was her poise. Rose moved with serene confidence, of belonging, of knowing who she was and what her destination in life was to be. Rose Mason was unlike anyone Rick had ever met. She was the epitome of everything that he had always hungered for but knew he could never attain: self-confidence and success.

The afternoon had been trouble from the beginning, with a sky turning dark and threatening around three o'clock. Leaden clouds hovered low and heavy above a choppy, angry ocean. Reed and Rick had been their busiest, warning families to keep children out of the surf, helping collapse umbrellas, catching runaway boards. Conditions were ripe for a major storm. The heat index had been in the '90s for the past week, and there had been rumors of a tropical depression off the Carolinas.

Rick could never figure out why Rose and her friend chose that afternoon to come to the lifeguards' stand and unroll their towels. He blamed it on the girlfriend. Was she hoping to lure Reed into an after-hours date? Rose was too smart to come out in weather this severe. She had told Rick that she had won some medals for swimming in college but he couldn't remember where. Surely Rose could see the danger in the raging water. Rick recalled the first crack of thunder and watching the lightning tear a jagged gash across the wet black ribbon of sky. It began to rain, pelting sheets of rain that stung like bullets. He remembered the fear - stark, stabbing, pulsating somersaults grinding in his gut.

At that moment Rose's friend ran into the water and started flailing her arms frantically among the foam and the waves. His first thought: "She's crazy." Nuts. No one should be in that stuff. He stood, paralyzed, rooted next to the lifeguards' stand. And then he saw Rose and Reed. They were shouting, running to the edge of the ocean and motioning. Reed dived into the water and swam towards a head that was still visible between cresting waves.

Now two heads were bobbing further and further away. Rose was standing there, looking back at him and screaming for Rick to come, to go in, to do *something*, to do *anything*. Then she collapsed on the wet and shifting shore. He remembered picking her up, cradling her in his arms, racing with her to the lifeguards' shed and lowering her gently on the cot they kept for emergencies. She didn't weigh more than a little kid. She looked so fragile, so innocent just lying there. Had she fainted or was she merely sleeping? How long had he knelt beside her? Couldn't have been more than five minutes because he panicked when he remembered Reed and the girl. Where were they? When he ran back to the shore he could see the beach patrol's boat racing toward a distant spot, its outboard motor a faint roar above the blast of the storm. The boat returned shortly with one body, that of Rose's girlfriend. Reed was forever lost to the ocean.

He stayed just long enough to assure himself that Rose was all right. He heard her cough, cry out for her friend (what was that girl's name?) and then the racking sobs as a gathering of onlookers tried comforting her. Rick made no attempt to crowd in and speak. His last memory of Rose Mason had been that of caressing her cheek with his fingers as he knelt beside her damp body. And now his odyssey had brought him back to her.

Rick Conklin vanished that July afternoon. Chicago, Minneapolis, Detroit. Always changing his address, his name, always finding new ways to stay alive. He was not chased by the law, indeed, had not committed any crime. At least in his eyes there was no crime.

Then why this cloud of guilt? There had been one wife and one divorce, then no more women. He found it impossible to get close to anyone, to feel tenderness toward man or woman. When memories crowded in and the two deaths haunted him, drink was a great eraser. But Rose Mason was a memory he did not want to erase.

For the past forty years, he had thought about Rose and the events of that afternoon. There were a lot of *what ifs*. *What if* he had been a hero, rescuing his buddy and Rose's girl friend? *What if*, despite the difference in age, Rose had been so overcome she would've come away with him? They could have made a life, a decent life, somewhere. Rick wondered if Rose's life had been as scarred by that afternoon as his had been. Would Rose even remember Virginia Beach in July 1961? Would she remember the young man who was afraid to leap into that roiling ocean and save her friend? Or would she remember only the fear that masked his face and paralyzed his legs? By flirting with the pretty young librarian in Detroit, Rick had traced Rose via the Internet to this retirement community. What was he seeking from Rose? Forgiveness? Acceptance? Understanding? A cushion of love to carry with him? Perhaps a little of each.

What sort of odds would the bookies give on east coast

beaches advertising for lifeguards twice in a half-century? And what would odds be on one man responding to that advertisement twice in a lifetime? Rick's life had changed forever on that afternoon in Virginia Beach. Now it was time to pick up the tenuous, looping strands of the past and confront his demons forever.

Rick Conklin Contemplates His Philosophies of Life

Damn! Hardest bed I've ever tried to sleep in. Carnival quarters had better pallets. Guess I'll just count the ceiling tiles and try to figure out what's what.

Okay. I'm in Virginia, Rose is in Virginia. Not ten miles away if that dumb clerk knows what he's talking about. *Wynfield Farms. Rose Mason.* Married to a *McNess.* McNess. But it's Rose Mason I remember. Man, she was a looker. Nice all the way through, guy could tell that at a glance. What am I going to say to her? Rose, I...Rose, I've been thinking about you all these years and...Rose, would you come to the beach again with me?

Oh hell, man, I ain't got a prayer. "Can you come to the beach with me and bring a wad of money, Rose? 'Cause I don't have a red cent to my name, and I won't until I get paid at the end of the week?" Nah, I don't want her to come see me at the beach. Just seeing her here will be enough. Rose is a once in lifetime sort of woman. Wonder if Ma was ever like that?

Don't go there, Rick, not back to Ma and Pop. No one ever said life was going to be a picnic. Life is what you make of the leftovers *after* the picnic.

4

For Rose, this morning has been an anodyne for her pain-ful confinement. Catching the drifts of conversation about the busy lives at Wynfield, she feels the tug on the line to get back in the swing of things. She understands Lib's concern about two of her favorite residents, but mostly she feels more like herself again.

Remembering, Rose smiles and thinks Bob Lesley was so welcoming and concerned for me. And Vinnie. And Jocey. Thank goodness I remembered to thank her for the flowers. And I *do* understand Lib's concern about Major Featherstone. He was in a real uproar about a newspaper article he'd read. But Charlie Caldwell had seen it too, so it wasn't a figment of the major's imagination.

Something about lifeguards not wanting to work. It really set Major Featherstone into a tizzy. I'll try to engage him in a game of checkers. That might calm his nerves and we can chat like the old friends we've always been.

How Frances carried on about the new residents who will be flooding into Wynfield soon. At least that kept her off the subject of David Heath-Nesbit! She is determined to con-jure up a romance between our guide and me. Rather clever how I steered her back to the cottages. It's hard to believe they're all sold. I'll never catch up with my interviews for *Wynsong*.

And dear Arthur, what did he say – 'I was beginning to act like a snoop?' Well, bully for me. That is exactly how I want to act! It's time I started poking around Wynfield Farms and found out what is really happening here.

Rose smiles to herself as she waits for Ellie to join her. Her friend is in rare form this morning, teasing Charlie about his broken hip last year in Oxford and threatening to post pictures of his swan dive into the Thames. Ellie certainly wasn't imbibing this morning, Rose concludes. Not a whiff, just like the rest of us.

"'Rose McNess, Snoop-At-Large.' Yes I like that." she chuckles.

"What are you laughing at Rose?" Ellie calls breathlessly as she puffs around the corner.

"Just thinking of resurrecting my career, Ellie – 'Rose McNess, Snoop.' You know it's my best role!"

"Whoopee! You don't know how good it is to hear you laugh again. Sorry I've kept you waiting; ready to ascend? I'll give you some clues for you first case as we go!"

Dr. Lesley's Reflections
On Major Featherstone's State of Mind

Never saw the old major as agitated as he was this morning. Can't believe he was all wrought up over that newspaper article. Rather, I can't believe that was the sole cause of his distress. And he was obviously distressed. Perhaps there's a health problem I don't know about. I'm not his doctor so, I'm not going to pry. That would violate medical ethics. I still believe in that even if I've been retired for more years than I can count. Could it be *Vinnie*? Is she the patient here? She certainly appears to be fine, never a hair out of place. Pretty as a debutante. I'll keep my eye on the old gentleman, challenge him to a game of chess next time we're together. He'd like that. Take his mind off whatever's bothering him.

5

Frances Keynes-Livingston stands sentry-straight beside the elevator. When Rose and Ellie arrive, she asks, in a voice capable of chilling a melon, "Ladies, shall we share the lift?"

"Absolutely," says Ellie. "I'll add my heft to it."

"Let's just say you're good ballast, Ellie," laughs Rose. "Actually, I think you've lost weight these past few weeks."

"She has, Rose. I can vouch for that. We're both at TWISTS three mornings a week. What did we decide to call ourselves, Ellie? 'The Leotard Ladies'?

"You got it, Frances. But 'Leotard *Loonies*' is more accurate. Rose, the instructor despairs of us. We talk so much we forget to listen to the tape. But I leave the gym feeling much better than when I entered. And when I had my checkup, the doctor said my heart rate has increased considerably, which is the reason I kill myself three times a week. Whoops! Here we are."

Rose pushes her walker onto the corridor. "Please stay and have a cup of tea. I've missed our chats, and I can't begin to tell you how good it is to laugh again. Please come in, even for a minute. I need to hear about TWISTS and all the other gossip we didn't cover down in the pub. Please say yes!"

"Oh, Rose," says Frances, "you must be tired. More

talk will exhaust you. A nap is what you need. Some other time, I promise."

"Frances is absolutely right, Rose. You don't want to overdo the first time," Ellie adds.

"Suppose I promise to *sit* and let you two wait on me? You'd be helping more than you realize."

Ellie and Frances laugh helplessly. "You always do get your way, Rose McNess. Oh, come on, Frances, let's help the old gal back to her playpen and then we can pilfer her pantry." Chuckling, the trio moves slowly toward Apartment 208.

"Sorry Max isn't here to greet us, ladies, but make yourselves at home. And pilfer away. I'm sure there are biscuits in the tin and Ellie knows where I keep tea and all the fixings. Now if you want some cheese—"

"Rose, stop giving orders or we shall leave this instant. We agreed to come in only if we could wait on you."

"I'll be quiet," replies a chastened Rose, adding meekly, "a cup of Earl Grey and a cracker for me. I admit that this exercise almost did me in. I'm pooped. As with everything in life, it's much easier going down than coming up."

Gingerly, fearfully, Rose lowers herself into the wing chair and pushes the walker to one side. "Heavenly. I may live after all."

"Oh goodie! I've found some of Tinnell's divine ham biscuits in your freezer, Rose. I'll heat these babies right up!"

The three friends settle themselves, a tea tray resting on the butler's table between them. Each sighs with contentment.

"This *was* a good idea, Rose. I'm glad you insisted."

"Think we should have asked Lib to join us?"

"Lib Everett? She has Arthur now. Besides, she's too damn cheerful."

"Since when is it offensive to be cheerful?"

"*You* know what I mean, Frances. She never looks grumpy or irritated or out of sorts. She *must* have some bad days. I admit it, I'm jealous."

"Ah ha! We've uncovered Ellie Johnson's cardinal sin,

the green-eyed monster of jealousy! Think we can live with that, Frances?" quips Rose.

"Forgiven. And forgotten. New subject. How did you think Vinnie looked?"

"Vinnie? As beautiful as ever. That porcelain-smooth skin is as fresh as a teenager's. And I've always said I've never seen such eyes. They're as blue as rare sapphires." Rose shook her head and conjured up a mental picture of Vinnie Featherstone, archetype of an old-fashioned Southern belle. "Why do I suspect you have something to add about Vinnie, Ellie?"

"Rose, we are all worried about both of them, especially the major. Did you notice anything, well, *different* about him this morning?"

Rose ponders Ellie's words. "Well, he did look a tad bit thinner. But remember, it has been nearly a month since I've seen him. Everyone changes. You're thinner too. And we are getting older. Lib had warned me that the major was a little fidgety. He did take off on lifeguards and working this morning. But Charlie saw the same article."

"Seems to me the more nervous he grows, the more composed Vinnie becomes."

"Acquiescence," sighs Frances Keynes-Livingston.

"Do they come to the pub every morning? Is *The Rose and The Grape* still a favorite gathering spot? If you tell me it is abused I just won't listen."

"Rose, for heaven's sake! You were there this morning! You saw how everyone enjoys this bit of socializing. You've been out of circulation a few weeks, not years! Why, the pub is the best thing that could have happened to Wynfield Farms. We all have you to thank for rallying us against Ms Moss and pushing it through. Don't you agree, Frances?"

"No question about it. It is the quiet hub of our lives as we regroup and retire."

"You should put that epithet into needlepoint, Frances," says Ellie. "'The quiet hub of our lives as we regroup and retire.' Yes, I like that. And sign it 'Thanks to Rose McNess'."

"You are both too kind. It took a united effort to bring the pub into being—united effort on the part of everyone at Wynfield. I'm just glad no one *overuses* it. Now, let's talk about TWISTS. Tell me all!" Rose places her teacup on the tray and leans forward towards her guests.

Ellie and Frances each explain the exercise franchise that has, with the Board's blessing, taken over an unused portion of the Wynfield Athletic Club.

"If we described each machine, Rose, you would think we were completely nuts. They are torture machines!"

"Torture us they may, Ellie, but you must add that they are approved for the over-sixty set and approved by the doctors *and* all the seniors' organizations, etc. The goal of the program is twofold. Strengthen muscles and elevate the heart rate. And it works."

"And we have fun doing it, Rose. You'll have to come."

"I'll come and *watch* for the duration, Ellie. I'm not making any plans until I get through this therapy. Talk about torture..."

"Exactly what kind of hip replacement did you have, Rose? I'm curious about the procedure," Frances matter-of-factly inquires.

"I opted for the adhesive procedure. Actually, I *had* no option. Dr. Sellsoe explained the different kinds before I went into surgery, but once he saw these old bones, he decided adhesive was the way to go. Said it should last eighteen to twenty years, provided I was careful on the tennis courts and ski slopes. I told him I'd give up playing singles and promised I wouldn't try out for the winter Olympics. If I'm around in twenty years, I'll go back for an update. Get the other hip tailored to match."

"If I were a betting woman, Rose, I'd put money on your being here in twenty years. I'm not so sure about that doctor."

"Your loyalty is touching, Ellie." Rose smiles at her friend, a true safeguard!

"Rose, you'll be interested to know there is one other

new program that has begun in your absence."

"What's that, Frances?"

"Sexology, 101."

"Frances! You're not serious—are you?"

"Dead serious, Rose. Ooops, 'dead serious' is not a good turn of phrase in this place, is it? But yes, Rose, they started this series last week. I believe the proper name is 'Senior Sociology' or something inane."

"But why? I mean, am I behind the times?"

Ellie sounds as if she is chirping as she says, "Only on this one thing, Rose. It's new to all of us."

"It seems," continues Frances, "that many of the residents' children are concerned about their parents fraternizing. Apparently some of our widowers invite ladies in for drinks—and a sleepover! And so the offspring have called Board members as well as Mrs. G., and they began this series last week."

"Well, I surely hope my children haven't called."

"Rose, your children are too enlightened; they wouldn't. Besides, they know you're helpless now. No one would dare take advantage of you"

"I don't know. If David Heath-Nesbitt came to town, they might have cause to worry."

"Stop it, you two. You're terrible. David and I are just good friends. How many times do I have to tell you that? And his grandchild is ill with something so drastic he cannot leave at this time."

"Aren't you just the teeniest bit disappointed, Rose? Come on, admit it."

"Oh, Ellie, I guess. But that would mean just one more person hanging about to wait on me. Let me get more mobile and then I'll welcome David. As a matter of fact, I plan to resume my regular walking schedule in the next few weeks."

"Speaking of walking, Rose," Frances chimes in, "any more travel plans in the future or is *Rose's Roamings* out of business?"

"Out of business? Frances, I'm indignant! Certainly not.

Of course, I won't be traveling far in the near future, but I've a yen to see Italy next spring. I long to drool over those melting Tuscan hills and sip wine in Firenze and Siena one more time. I've already talked to David and he is wildly enthusiastic. Said that late March is ideal, before tourists invade the countryside and spring colors are at their peak. How does that sound, fellow travelers, 'Italy in the Spring'?"

"Rose, you're too much! Here you sit, major surgery merely weeks ago and already planning another trip. As your former roommate in London, may I sign up this instant for *the* same role in Italy? I don't care where we go; I'll be on that plane." Ellie sits back and grins foolishly, elated at the thought of Rose's plans.

"Speaking of London," Frances begins cautiously. "I must ask you two for advice."

"You're in the presence of two experts, dearie. Shoot."

"The doctor I met in Chelsea Hospital, my colleague, Dr. Evan Wickham-Biggs, has asked me to join him in Australia in late August. I was wondering ..."

The Main Line Matron is not allowed to finish.

"Frances! You sneak! Holding out on us, huh? You've been in touch with that lovely man you met in London?" Ellie poses this as a question but she has already guessed the answer.

"Evan is head of the biological research team at Chelsea Hospital and has done all sorts of exciting work on lichens throughout the world."

"But how wonderful," exclaims Rose. "Two like minds interested in the same subject, albeit a subject alien to the rest of us mortals. This is the best possible news you could give me on my road to recovery, Frances."

Normally a stoic, inward-thinking woman, Frances visibly relaxes with Rose's accolade of approval. "You don't think I'm foolish at my age? Going half-way around the world to see him? "

"Foolish?" cries Ellie. "Girl, you gotta grab life when it happens. If this doctor is as nice as Rose and I suspect, you're one lucky lady. Go for it! If I were in your shoes, I'd already be applying for British citizenship. And speaking of shoes, tell me you didn't wear those gosh-awful boats this past trip."

Ellie glances at Rose and they exchange a moment of subtle eye rolling. Both were thinking of the thigh-high brown lace-ups with inch thick yellow soles that Frances wore exclusively throughout *Rose's Roamings.*

"Ha! Evan said that was what attracted him to me— my shoes! He told me that at last he had met an American woman who knew how to dress properly for English weather."

"What a couple you'll make! I can hear the official presenting you to the Queen, Mrs. Frances Keynes-Livingston and Dr. Evan Wickham-Biggs, eminent lichenologists and students of *love."*

"Now Ellie, don't make me sorry I told you about Evan. Since you're practically packing my bag for down under, tell me what I should do about Maine. My children expect me to join them there in August. As I've always done."

"Honey, you tell them the truth," commands Ellie. "If they are a bit prudish, tell them more about the meeting than the man. Then casually slip in the fact that this famous doctor asked you to join him there. You know, blah, blah, blah. And say, 'So sorry, the lobsters will have to do without me this year'."

"My sentiments precisely, Ellie," marvels Rose with a knowing smile.

"Thank you, my friends. And I mean that sincerely. It's good to be able to talk about Evan. I've longed to confide in someone —someone I can trust. I appreciate your advice because I value your friendship so very much."

Frances allows herself to slip into the past for a moment. Dare she tell her two close friends how, with Evan, she had found real love? How loving him had made the years with her ex-husband seem shallow and cheap? She counted the number of years she had been the dutiful wife in Ardmore, chairing garden clubs, raising three children, organizing church benefits, and making excuses for Mr. Ned the no-show. Forty-one wasted years. Why had she finally snapped? She almost laughed. Of course, it was Ned asking if she minded him bringing his secretary to the Club picnic because he was going do a lot of work afterwards. That tart! How surprised he looked when she announced that he could work at home because it was not *their* home anymore— she was leaving immediately. And now she had Evan, who loved her and desired her. Yes, *desired* her old and wrinkled body. What did Ellie just say? 'Go for it!' By damn, I shall!

Rose watches the thin, patrician woman with keen eyes and thinks that this has not been easy for Frances. Neither telling Ellie and me about her male friend nor asking for advice. For once, she does not control the situation; for once, she has reached out for help. How foolish we mortals really are! Every captain needs a second mate for safety.

"Now it's my turn to ask for advice," admits Rose sheepishly. Her companions settle their teacups and prepare to listen.

"It is nothing exciting, like Frances's news. It's just, just that, well I need to ask you something. About my forgetfulness."

The two ladies roar, and fairly shout at Rose, "Is that all?"

"You laugh now, but wait. Ellie, would you look in that drawer behind you? That's it. See the envelope? Hand it to me, if you will."

Ellie turns to the small table behind her chair and does as she is told.

"Thanks. Now listen, you two, to my latest bout of forgetfulness. This letter came while I was in Assisted Living. Postmarked Ohio. Toledo, I think. How many weeks ago was that? Three? I stuffed it into the pocket of my robe and forgot it. Completely! Until yesterday. Let me read this and you tell me what you think."

Rose reads the letter to her friends as they sit expectantly, silently. When she finishes, Frances speaks first. "Didn't you say you did quite a bit of traveling Rose? Before you settled down to teach? This is obviously someone from your past trying to be relevant to your present."

"But who is this person? I've racked my brain since yesterday wondering who Rick Conklin is and what old times he is talking about. My forgetfulness is depressing. I had too much time in Assisted Living, lying there and thinking, just thinking, and realizing I was getting older by the minute. I tell you ladies, I don't like feeling frail or less than fit. And I *do not like* forgetting a Mr. Rick Conklin, who writes this personal letter."

"Probably an old beau, possibly from college. I'm with Frances. I bet he is from your swinging era, Rose. Why should you remember him? He was a mere blip on your screen way back when."

"Thank you, ladies. You've lifted my spirits. Could be someone I met at one of those awful mixers in Boston. I won't give him another thought. Now, quickly, fill me in on any other news. Has Mrs. Gallentine-rhymes-with-Valentine been treating everyone well? Personally I have more respect for her each passing day. She shows everyone great kindness, equally as gracious to the staff as she is to the residents."

"She is an innately good woman," Frances adds. "Did you know that she is *Dr.* Gallentine?"

"No!" sing Rose and Ellie, speaking almost in unison. Both look stunned at this revelation.

"Indeed. Undergraduate degree from Goucher College, then Master's and Ph.D. from either American University or the University of Georgia. For the life of me I can't remember which university."

"Your amnesia is contagious, Rose," jokes Ellie.

Laughing, Rose says, "I am impressed. But regardless of all the degrees, Paula Gallentine is a wonderful Resident Director. I like the way she introduces the new residents into the routine of the dining room and the few changes she has made in the reception hall. Yes, Mrs. Gallentine is a keeper. Any idea of *her* past life? She's a widow, I heard that early on."

"She keeps very close-mouthed about her personal life.

Whoever her husband was, I just hope he was as handsome and smart as she."

"She has a bit of a mystery on her hands now. You know how fastidious she is. Well, I mean you can *tell* by the way she dresses, always up-to-the-minute elegant even on Saturday mornings."

"Nothing mysterious about that," opines Rose. "That's just the way she is."

"I mean the blurb in *Wynsong* this week. Did you read it?"

Puzzled, Rose shakes her head, "No."

"Mrs. Gallentine has found bundles of trash hidden in isolated corners of the hallways."

"I read that, Ellie, but is there something more ominous there other than a closet slob among us?" Frances's expression is as puzzled as Rose's.

"A slob playing with matches *is* ominous if you ask me," Ellie adds decisively. "Of course the matches had all been burned, but I still don't like it. A fire in this old place would be disastrous. This house is a potential tinder box, even with sprinklers in place."

The three residents let the impact of Ellie's words sink in.

Again Frances speaks first, "I have utmost confidence in Mrs. Gallentine. Finding the trash shows what a sharp eye she keeps on every corner of Wynfield Farms. Why, I bet anyone of us would have walked right over such a bundle two or three times a day. Yes, I definitely feel Mrs. Gallentine is on top of this situation. *If* it's a situation at all. Could be one of the painters forgetting to pick up his stuff when he leaves for the day."

"Well, I agree with Ellie's original premise: our Resident Director has a bit of a mystery on her hands. Too bad I'm not quite up to my usual snooping," Rose laughs. "You know how I love to dig up the dirt!"

"Well, no digging today, Miss Marple. We have overstayed our welcome. Ellie and I are going to wash up and leave things to drain. No leftovers. We finished all the cheese *and* biscuits. Can you manage the bed? I'd be happy to see you tucked in."

"Shoo! You and Ellie go on. I've taken too much of your time, but golly, wasn't it fun? It feels so good to laugh again."

"You know what they say about laughter and medicine," chortles Ellie. "You've done *us* good, Rose, just being around *you.*"

"You have fed my soul and my body— literally a communion of spirits. But wait, I want to ask you about Jana. Is it true about precious Fleur?"

"Sadly true," confesses Ellie. "I was hoping you wouldn't ask. But don't weep for Jana. She called a friend and they went out the day after Fleur's demise and returned with a two-year-old poodle named Lucy. Cute as a button. Jana is absolutely smitten."

Rose laughs at the thought of this. "Won't Max have a time? Maybe he'll be nicer to Lucy than he was to Fleur. Any other news I simply have to know?"

"Rose," implores Ellie, "will you please take your phone off the hook, retire to your bedroom, and go to bed? Let me take your wastebasket. That still signifies 'DO NOT DISTURB' does it not?"

"Right, Ellie. Goodbye to both of you. I shall head for dreamland. There really is just so much news one can absorb over a cup of tea."

Frances Keynes-Livingston Breathes a
Great Sigh of Relief After Baring Her Soul

I cannot believe that I told Rose and Ellie about Evan! And they did seem, well, understanding. A beau at my age! Even I find that absurd! I wish I were as impetuous as Ellie. What did she say—'go for it!' That is definitely not my philosophy, Ellie Johnson. But I'm doing all right, thank you very much! I shall place a call to Evan the moment I reach my apartment, tell him to firm up plans for Australia this week. Maine will simply have to do without me this year!

If only Rose's recuperation were as simple as my romance. That strange letter is surely a puzzle. She has been getting a bit fuzzy in the memory department, but who am I to talk?

Now let me see, U.K. time is six hours ahead of ours, so if it is one o'clock here...

6

Rose is not tired. She dutifully moves into the bedroom, climbs onto her bed, and gropes for the second pillow. Ummm, have I a pen and notepad? Rose sits up, turns to her bedside table, and fishes in the drawer for ever-ready supplies. A good reporter is never without tools of the trade.

Now I've got two mysteries on my hands. Better get busy. *Get over this hip and get busy.* What about this Rick Conklin? Perhaps Annie may remember my mentioning him. There really is no one else to ask. And as for the trash problem, I might be able to help. I can prowl the hallways with my walker and scour every corner. I'm sure one of the painters left it, probably in a rush and knew it would be picked up eventually. But the boxes of spent matches add a mysterious touch. I need to speak to Mrs. G. She was so kind in helping Annie keep this apartment spic and span.

My goodness, so much to remember. I'm too wrought up to nap. What a newsy pair! I better make a to-do list.

ELLIE: Should I speak to her? No drinking this morning. I'll wait on that. Lib may have been overreacting because she's such a teetotaler. Or is she? Anyway, POSTPONE—Ellie.
MAJOR FEATHERSTONE: This is a dilemma. He and Vinnie are so devoted. Observe— that's all anyone can

do. Nothing worse than a meddler. I'll seek him out when I'm downstairs. I'll get him in that checkers game, ask him questions about his military experience, and his opinion on Iraq. I can flatter the major. He probably knows so much about our country's defense and security that he's frustrated in not being able to do anything.

JANA: I can hardly wait to see Jana and her new dog. What was its name? Molly? A female, I remember that. Misty? Oh bother, I certainly don't need to keep that in my mind. New poodle and that's that.

MRS. GALLENTINE: Definitely need to talk to Mrs. Gallentine, I wonder what her husband was like ...

Paula Gallentine, the person Rose needs to talk to, is a tall woman. She stands at her desk and stretches to her full height of six feet one. She needs this stretch to relieve the kinks in her calves and her mind. Hearty ancestors gave Paula long limbs, broad shoulders, and a strong carriage that bows to no one. Her coffee-color skin is as smooth and silky as the nylons she invariably wears on her elegant legs. People notice Paula's legs, once they look past her face.

She has a broad, smooth forehead fringed by loopy ringlets that she occasionally attacks with fingernail scissors. Large topaz eyes—shimmering to quartz or bronze depending on Paula's emotions—look straight ahead, unafraid of what they may or may not encounter. High, photo-perfect cheekbones and a straight nose that is actually too long and too narrow for her broad face complete the path to Paula's mouth which, when open in a smile, reveals a set of exquisite white teeth as precious as a strand of pearls from Tiffany's.

When Paula Gallentine smiles, audiences melt and grown men tremble. When it was announced that this paragon of brains and beauty was coming to Wynfield Farms to replace the martinet Miss Moss, many called her foolish, a bitter young widow, and token Black. But no one denied that she was formidable in every way and a force that the retirement community would soon recognize as one of their most fortuitous assets.

Mrs. Gallentine sighs and wiggles her fingers. She covers the files on her desk with *Alive at Sixty-Five!* and strides into the main hall. Patient, she waits as the receptionist finishes a phone conversation, then announces, in a throaty voice that seems to invite conspiracy, "Miss Mueller, I'm going to take a long walk. If there are messages say that I shall return after two. I'll be happy to return calls after that time."

"Of course, Mrs. Gallentine. Back after two. I understand."

"Anything for me to sign before I go?"

"Nothing that can't wait. I'm trying to get the cottage contracts processed so you can look them over. Hopefully, they'll be ready for you to sign and send out in one mailing."

"Very efficient, Karen. All right, I'm off."

Jacqueline Paula Marceline Kincaid Gallentine gives the plump receptionist a sincere smile, turns on sensible heels and walks through the impressive front doors of Wynfield Farms.

She hugs the beige cashmere cardigan to fend off a late April breeze that is cooler than she had anticipated. Smiling, she reflects on what she has just done. Thirty years ago I would never have walked through those front doors. 'Course thirty years ago this wasn't a home for seniors, much less a retirement community. Even so, Jacqueline Paula Marceline Kincaid would have left through the kitchen door, or the service door in the health wing. That is, if I had landed a job here at the Big House. Probably didn't hire Negroes back then. Too many hardworking farm folks for these posh jobs. Just like Karen. Solid, plodding honest Karen. I can train her if she stays long enough.

She reflects once more on the simple act of walking through Wynfield Farms' front door. Time has been kind to you, Jacqueline Paula Marceline.

It is noon. Lunch is a meal she seldom eats, so the next two hours are hers to squander. And today, in a spring sun both coy and beckoning, she desires only to explore the gardens and grounds and yes, perhaps even the narrow side roads that parallel the Wynfield property.

I do love this place, she thinks. After barely a year, I cannot imagine being anywhere else. My apartment is small but what more do I need? And this position is all that I had prayed it might be. Just hope the Board keeps giving me positive ratings. As I said in March, I'm generally a happy person and I like a happy work place. As long as folks understand my style, we'll get along just fine.

Again she smiles and stops on the Monet Bridge. The clear steam gurgles and bubbles, flowing swiftly to the distant lake. She stops and listens. Noises of both stream and birds provide cheerful exclamation points to the hush of the April afternoon. Paula's thoughts traverse the past forty-one years.

My life has been like this creek, twisting, turning, pouring over rocks and boulders and spilling into a pond. Only my pond is Wynfield Farms and I call that a pretty good landing.

Paula had been the third of six children born to Alma and Wesley Kincaid. Her mother worked the night shift at Kroger Bakery, bringing home a modest wage and bags of day-old breadstuffs. Paula stopped and inhaled deeply. She could almost smell the sweet yeasty odors of the rolls and soft loaves that were dumped on the kitchen table each night; hunger was never a guest in the Kincaid home. Her father was a drifter, drifting in long enough to get Alma pregnant and then drifting out again. After the sixth child, a little boy who died at three months, Wesley vanished from their lives. His leaving was etched in Paula's mind.

"Can I see what you got Daddy?" she asked, jumping to reach into the greasy pockets of his one jacket. Occasionally she found a penny, a dime, or sometimes her favorite, a peppermint.

"Not today, sugar, Daddy's goin' to need his dimes for the trolley."

"Not no trolleys in Roanoke, Daddy," Emmeline had piped.

"Where I'm goin' there's trolleys," he replied.

"Where's that, Daddy?"

"For me to know and you to find out. You kids be good to your mama. I'll send you a postcard when I get to where I'm goin'."

With this, Wesley Kincaid walked out of the house. Paula had reported the conversation to her mother that evening. Alma merely nodded, straightened tired shoulders, and headed for the kitchen to pour herself the cup of coffee that Paula knew to have ready.

Paula had been eight. Soon afterward her two older brothers left for Tennessee to live with Mama's sister Tess. Paula understood that they had taken to farm life and she never heard from them again. She assumed the care of the younger girls, Emmeline and Casey, making sure they wore clean clothes to school and finished their homework when they returned after school. They got along just fine. Emm and Casey, both married and moved to California before they were eighteen; who knows what they're doing now. And Mama, bless her, died before she knew I was going to be a *Somebody*. I was almost there, Mama, almost there! Mama, if you were alive today I'd bring you out to Wynfield Farms and put you in one of these fancy apartments. I'd keep you like a cat in cream.

Miss Kerns, her high school English teacher, was a stereotype spinster with the acuity to discern the spark of knowledge in young Jacqueline Paula Marceline Kincaid. This was the spark that exceptional teachers yearn to discover and ignite in one rare student.

Miss Kerns spared nothing in her zeal, personally arranging for interviews with and scholarships to Goucher College. Jacqueline excelled. Miss Kerns encouraged her protégé's efforts to attend graduate school and dipped into her personal savings to help finance Jacqueline's first year at American University.

And it was Miss Kerns who gently suggested dropping either her first or third Christian name for scholarly reasons. ("*When you publish your first papers, my dear, one name, and I suggest 'Paula'. This followed by the surname 'Kincaid' is sufficient, professional and impressive.*")

At first, Paula resented Miss Kern's suggestion. By then she was fairly sick of being coached, bossed, and cajoled by the powdery spinster with the large bosom. Sick, even, of having to depend on her for financial support. But she relented and soon was profoundly grateful. For the past ten, twenty, years, 'Paula' she had been. The papers were published and her recognition as an outstanding geriatric sociologist was heralded.

Sadly, Miss Kerns had died while Paula was in the "ABCD" ("All But Completing Dissertation") phase of her Ph.D. at Georgia State. Paula remained in Atlanta to teach at Spelman College. She returned home at her mother's sudden death and learned the family home had been left solely to her. The house was a four-over-four brick in a decent section of town. The realtor who came to appraise it was a light-skinned Negro named Andre Gallentine. He was the most handsome man Paula had ever seen. Not that she had been squinting at many men during the past ten years of grinding academia. When they went upstairs to look at the bedrooms it was almost dark, and the lust and lovemaking that erupted seemed the most natural occurrence in the world—romantic, violent, forceful, charged with unknown passions. It amazed them both, and, drained and depleted, they lay on Paula's childhood bed and marveled at the wonder of it all.

"We'll get married!" Andre had whispered. "Tomorrow. I got to have you in my life."

"I hardly know you," Paula blurted. "I don't know what's come over me. I've never done this in my life."

"But you love it, don't you gal? How tall are you? Six feet? More?"

"Six-one. My daddy was tall."

"Man, I could wrap you 'round me twice. You one luscious peach."

Paula submitted her resignation to Spelman, effective immediately, and they were married. Jacqueline Paula Marceline Kincaid became the prize and pride of Andre Gallentine. He kept his wife in fine clothes and a new car and issued the edict that "No wife of mine is going to work outside the house."

The sheer contentment of belonging to someone who loved her wholly was enough for Paula. For a while. She enjoyed the freedom of her days and the wild lovemaking of their nights. Two years into the marriage Andre, hurrying up the steps of the Roanoke courthouse to record a real estate deed, suffered a massive heart attack and died.

Paula's heart was broken. Andre had been good for her. Months passed before she left the house, even to shop or go to the cleaners. She had few friends, no family to comfort her. She thought often about her mama and how she must have felt when Wesley left. One afternoon she idly flipped through the pages of *The Roanoke Times*.

The advertisement read "Position for Resident Director...nice place to live, salary to be determined, interaction with senior citizens in rural residential community." What could be more perfect? Her predecessor had not been overly friendly, but she had been impressed with Paula's resume and requested that she return to meet the Board of Directors. Paula was interviewed and offered the job. She accepted the position with the provision that she would report in two weeks. That had been April of last year.

Almost a year to the day, she remembers fondly.

Paula walks on, following the serpentine path and making mental notes for Romero. I must get him to clean those leaves from the bank. Also, the roots should be removed. Probably the ones that tripped Mrs. McNess a few weeks back.

She thinks about the two incidents with the matches in the bundles of trash. Did Wynfield simply have a careless litterbug? Or could it be something—or someone—who is a potential threat? Some of her seniors are so vulnerable. She dismisses such a thought as one of her crazier, more paranoid ideas.

Her mind racing, Paula recalls the deskwork and decisions she has momentarily left behind. Construction of the twelve cottages is on schedule and the architects have met with the Board and Jocey to discuss the landscaping in the area.

That is going to be a muddy mess for months. Nothing I can do about that! Will the new seniors join in the house activities? Or keep to themselves in a tight cluster? I've got to prevent that because it can happen.

The Japanese sociologists! How could *that* slip my mind? I'm sure it's on the calendar but I better start planning now. I'll call Dr. Becker first thing and check on the number. He said we were the last stop before they flew home. How many on the tour? Forty? Forty-four? I'll need volunteers to hostess and I better speak to Chef Leon about a simple lunch. And flowers. Yes, definitely special centerpieces.

Preoccupied with calculating the logistics for a busload of visitors, Paula rounds a blind corner and bumps into Jocey Ribble, deep into a huge boxwood. Only her denim-clad legs are visible, giving her the semblance of a prickly green hedgehog. The two women jump and speak at once.

Paula laughs and says, "Jocey! I'm so sorry. Did I push you into that shrub? I apologize. I was lost in my thoughts."

Jocey giggles and shakes boxwood leaves from her overall bib. "No, no, Mrs. Gallentine. I'm out here doing what I should have been doing all last week, peeping the boxwood. You have to get right in the middle of these big ones to do it properly."

"Whatever it is you're doing, they look wonderful. I take it 'peeping' means pruning down inside, correct?"

"Absolutely, Mrs. Gallentine. Not many folks know that. Did you realize Thomas Jefferson brought this technique to America from France in the 18th century? Think he was our first 'peeping Tom'?"

"I certainly didn't know that. In fact, I can't even think

where I first heard the term 'peeping'. Probably from grounds men at Spelman. But enough about boxwood. I was thinking of you when we crashed. I'm going to need some stunning table arrangements for a luncheon next week. I'll have to check the date, but we have a busload of Japanese sociologists coming to Wynfield Farms and of course they're invited for lunch. If I give you the exact day and time, think you can whip up something marvelous for me?"

Jocey agrees enthusiastically. "No problem. I like doing the extras. Gives me a chance to experiment. I'll come up with an Oriental design. Simple but elegant."

"Anything you do will be lovely. I've enjoyed your talents for a year. You have magic in your fingertips. You turn the Wynfield canvas from drab to dramatic. I mean that."

Jocey blushes and shakes more leaves from her dark hair. "Sure is a shame Dr. Stoneman just died. He would love to greet the Japanese, and probably show off his *bonsai.*"

"You've just reminded me of something else. Hostesses. Be thinking, will you, of residents you think would enjoy the role of host or hostess."

"There's none better than Mrs. McNess. Think she'd do it, Mrs. Gallentine?"

"I'd hesitate to ask her. It's has been only weeks since her accident and surgery. I'll have to think about that," considers Mrs. Gallentine.

"Shoot! If they're not coming until next week, she'll be up for it. That little lady hates to be left out of *anything.* Bet if you ask her, then Mrs. Johnson and the double name lady will be happy to help. And why not Mrs. Stoneman? She could tell the Japanese about her husband's hobby."

"Jocey, you're a goldmine today. Keep thinking, I like all of your suggestions." Paula glances at her watch. "Would you look at the time? Good heavens, almost two. I've got to run, but we'll talk later. If you don't hear from me, stop by the office. My door is always open."

And that, thinks Jocey, is exactly why everyone at Wynfield Farms has taken to you. No hiding away in that fancy paneled office like Miss Moss.

Paula waves and starts walking briskly back to her commitments.

"Well, Lord," she whispers aloud, "I've spent a good two hours rewinding my life's tape for You. Forgive me for my misdoings. Like not getting the family together for Mama's funeral. But if the Red Cross and the Internet couldn't locate them, what's a girl to do? Should I have tried harder? They all must be better off than I am. Or dead. I did the best I could. But thank you, thank you for all you've given me in this life: Mama, Miss Kerns, and especially, Andre. And this job. No, Lord, this *position*. And now, I'll get on back to whatever you call it, job *or* position. After I take the long way home, if you don't mind."

Nearly two! Now what will Miss Karen Mueller do if I don't show up precisely at two. Why didn't I bring an apple out here with me? Suddenly I'm hungry. And thinking about Mama makes me remember all those good things she cooked for us kids. How in Sam Hill did she do it? Those were real dinners we ate, all of us around that old oak table, dishing up bowls of salad, potatoes, fighting over the last piece of pie. How many bags of day-old bread did she drag in? Sticky buns, pecan twists, French rolls, ummmm. Listen to my stomach growl. Wonder we didn't get as fat as ten little pigs. And oh, that Tomato Pie. Wonder if Chef could try that? What was Mama's recipe?

1 quart home canned tomatoes—drain and save the juice
Half loaf stale white bread, torn in bits
Onion, chopped, if you got it
2-3 dabs real butter
salt & pepper & handful brown sugar
Mix all together and bake 'till bubbly in greased pan.

Now chef will ask how hot the oven should be, exactly how *much* brown sugar, but Lord, I don't know! Mama never measured, she just *knew*. And I know one thing for sure, there's never any leftovers from Mama's Tomato Pie. I'm going straight to Chef Leon and see if he knows anything about making puddings from tomatoes. And maybe he'll let me sneak some leftover salad. Good old days of potatoes and rolls are done and gone, Paula Gallentine.

WYNFIELD FARMS
Retirement community

Wynfield Farms Retirement Community has been honored as one of twelve retirement communities in the country to play host to a contingent of visiting Japanese sociologists. The group of approximately forty-three men and women has been sent here by their government to study how the U.S. cares for its senior population. Our home is the final stop on their two-week tour and we hope that they leave us concluding that they have "saved the best for last". We expect our guests to arrive at 11:00 A.M. on the morning of May 7. Miss Mueller and I shall be calling upon several of you to act as guides both in the gardens and throughout the house. I hope that if you are tapped for such a duty you will say 'Yes.' Both our guests and residents will be welcomed to a festive luncheon in the Wynfield Dining Room at 1:00 P.M. I hope you will look forward to this occasion as much as I am.

Paula Gallentine
Resident Director

To her surprise, Rose did nap. She remembers looking at the clock at 1:10 and the next time it was 4:00.

Let's face it, Rose McNess, you are a pathetic invalid. I don't even call that a nap. More like deep slumber. I feel much better, though. The doctors are right. Everything in moderation and plenty of rest. Such a bore! I have been reduced to talking to myself! I can't wait to get Max home. At least he listens, and I don't sound like a babbling idiot to him.

Rose sits in front of the mirror in her bedroom and brushes her short hair with vigorous, decisive strokes. She inspects her forehead. Good, that bruise is fading to a paler shade of yellow. No stitches, thank heavens. The ringing of the phone cuts short her *toilette*.

"Oh bother! I'll have to hustle and get it. How do people know when I'm not close to the telephone? Hold on, I'm coming I'm coming ..."

"Hello? Mrs. Gallentine! How nice to hear your voice. Yes, I am getting stronger each day. And *thank you* for seeing that my apartment was spotless when I returned. I am tardy in expressing my gratitude. Yes, everything was perfect." A long pause. "Next Thursday? I don't know why not. Of course I'll be feeling up to it if you give me *inside* duty. With Jana? Oh, perfect. And I'll be particularly interested in meeting the Japanese. You do know that my grandson Tom and his bride are living..." Pause. "Of course, I guess I've told everyone in Wynfield about them. Absolutely, put me down as tour guide. I'll be delighted. Good bye to you, too."

That will be an interesting day. A busload of Japanese sociologists visiting Wynfield Farms. I'm thrilled Mrs. Gallentine called me. I'll work hard at therapy every day so I'll be fit for Thursday. I shall make myself get up for the occasion.

Rose is debating about changing into a fresh blouse when a rap on her door stops her. No time to freshen up. Whoever it is will take me as I am. "Coming!"

She opens the door to find the Puffenbarger twins standing in the hallway. They wear sheepish expressions "I told sister we should have called first," begins Henrietta.

"But if we had called, the phone would have disturbed you, so I said 'Let's just go, sister'," finishes Harriet.

"Henrietta Cora and Harriet Alberta! Come in this minute. You two are a double sight for my sore eyes!"

"Rose, do you know that you are the only person in this place that knows our middle names? And even uses them?"

"Well of course I know them. I interviewed you for *Wynsong*, remember? However, I do lose track of a lot of things, you understand."

"Don't we all?" the twins agree.

"You must tell me how the opera season was the past few months, Henrietta. Did you get to listen to all your old favorites?" Posing this question to Henrietta, Rose fervently hopes she has pegged the correct twin as music lover.

"Indeed I did, Rose. Thank you for asking. We shall miss Pavarotti this next season, but the new man coming along seems promising."

Bingo! Henrietta is the musician. That means Harriet is the sportswoman.

"And Harriet, how is your golf game this spring?"

"I'm slowing down, Rose. Doctor's orders. He's restricted me to nine holes."

Henrietta interjects, "But nine holes four times a week equals two eighteen hole games. If my math is correct, sister."

Rose cannot stifle a giggle. "You two! I feel like a slacker just listening to you! Oh, how I wish I could walk that course with you, Harriet. But I shall. I promise. This hip is *not* going to be the end of me."

"That is what we have ascertained for ourselves, Rose. And I know I speak for sister in saying that you look well. As my dear mother would say, 'you are blooming'. Isn't that right, sister?"

"Blooming more than poor Esther Jenkins. Tell her about Esther, sister."

In a tone deep and lugubrious, Henrietta begins a long tale of Esther Jenkins' collapse on the patio of the music room two days ago. Rose fears the twin is going to recount every hour since the poor woman's demise when Harriet neatly finishes the story.

"Esther is now in her own bed recovering from a mild stroke and being cared for by a licensed practical nurse that Bob Jenkins hired from some private agency."

"And Bob, don't forget the part about Bob, sister. They say he sits and holds her hand and reads poetry to her," adds Henrietta, determined to conclude the Jenkins saga in her own words.

"I'm sorry to hear that," Rose sympathizes. "About the *stroke*, I mean. The Jenkins are quite a duo. Remember how they tramped the streets of London and Cambridge with us? Talk about a surprise!"

They all break out in laughter over thoughts of last year's travels. Each woman's thoughts return to a favorite snapshot in her own album of memories. For Rose it is Cambridge, with twisting streets and serene spires. Harriet shudders at the thought of her night in the V & A, lost and alone in that cavernous mausoleum. Henrietta closes her eyes and smiles as she recalls a cream tea at Brown's.

"Harriet, where are our manners?"

"I've brought you some of Harriet's fresh apple muffins, Rose. As we were passing the lobby, mail arrived, so we brought yours up. No sense in your making a trip when we were coming, isn't that right, sister?"

"Thank you so much, ladies. I do love Harriet's muffins. They shall probably be my supper. And you're right, I made my initial foray downstairs this morning and I was flat out by noon. One trip a day is definitely sufficient. Just leave the mail on the table if you don't mind. Now, may I offer you a cup of tea?"

The twins rise as one and demur, finishing each other's sentences and insisting that they have time limits for visiting the sick and would you look? They have already overstayed their fifteen minutes and yes, sister, it indeed is time to go. And we promised Father Charlie that we would feed Caesar this afternoon so they must hurry along and hope the drop-in visit wasn't too upsetting for Rose who should not get up, absolutely not, we shall see ourselves out.

Which they do. Rose sits in her favorite chair and chuckles until she's weak.

My favorite twins. They are truly cut from the same bolt of cloth. They think the same thoughts, finish each other's sentences, probably dream the same dreams. I shudder to think of one going...No, I will not go there. Where did they leave the mail?

Rose picks up the collection of letters and catalogues and returns to her seat by the window. "I don't think I'll be needing a new bathing suit this season," she mutters, dropping the slick catalogue into the trash bin that Henrietta had brought in from the hallway. What is this? Uh oh, Medicare bill. That goes in the pile with all the others. Oh, a note from Paul. My son has inherited my poor handwriting, poor guy. In this age of e-mail and cell phones, I guess I'm lucky to receive handwritten word from either of my boys. No, I'm not going to castigate you for your illegible scrawl, son. You came by it honestly.

Dear Ma,April 20
I'm the DW (designated writer) for Rob
and me. Glad to get your letter last week.
Don't spend too much time at the computer
though—your hip really will suffer!
 All of us are fine here. Sue's office is
going through a transition but looks as
if her job is o.k. Let's hope. Boys are
busy with schoolwork and usual activities—swimming lessons, Cub Scouts, and
now spring soccer starts in 3 weeks. I
gather Rob's family is doing the same
thing; we are all going in different directions at the same time.
 Annie says Max has settled in nicely.
Please don't bring him back to Wynfield
too soon as you should not try to walk him
yet! Will try to call this weekend.
 Love ya,
 Paul

The third piece of mail is so badly wrinkled it looks as
if it had been run over by the mail truck not one, but two or
three times. The envelope is small and ordinary, the kind
people use to pay their bills.

Rose scans the postmark: Reading, Pennsylvania. Mysterious! I don't know a soul in Reading. Did I send in a cou-
pon for a rebate? No, those places are usually out in Iowa or
Colorado. A real puzzle. Certainly looks like a rebate envelope. There is only one way to find out. Rose slits the top and
pulls out a single sheet of thin blue paper. Smoothing it on
the arm of the chair and she reads:

Dear Rose,
 I am almost in Virgnia. Wow. Pretty country around here. Do you think you and Me could
eat together? I would really like to talk over

```
old times. I have some good News to tell you
about my new job. Hope you're doing fine and
I'll see you soon.
          Your friend from long ago,
          Rick
```

Rose is as still as a stone. She stares at the message in front of her: *Can't even spell Virginia.* Her emotions range from bewilderment, dismay, curiosity, and yes, unease. She pounds her head in frustration. Why can't I place this creature? *Who* is Rick? Where in the world would I have met him? 'A friend from long ago.' High school? Well, if that is the case it is impertinent of him to even think I remember who he is. 'New job?' Why should I be interested in his new job if I can't remember his old one? If it weren't for the postmarks, I'd say it was a prank. My friends wouldn't do this to me. Who has time for such foolishness?

Unless this character is crawling on all fours, he's undoubtedly in Virginia right now. Reading, Pennsylvania is *not* that far away. This is all very unsettling. I'm not prone to fears or phobias or worries about matters I cannot change. But this letter and the fact that behind the letter is a person who knows me, is definitely disturbing. This is how I felt after September 11— unhinged and unglued. Wonder if Doctor Selby could give me something…*not* Selby: there I go again. Whatever; his name begins with a 'S'. Perhaps a tranquilizer? Then I'd really be in la-la land. Rick, Rick, Rick. I don't know anyone named *Rick*.

Rose carefully reinserts the letter into the battered envelope and places it in the drawer with the first one.

There, Rick whoever. I shall deal with you later.

"...I pray you, in your letters,
When you shall these unlucky deeds relate,
Speak of me as I am; nothing extenuate,
Nor set down aught in malice: then must you speak
Of one that lov'd not wisely but too well;..."

  Shakespeare, *Othello*, act V, scene ii
  William Shakespeare

8

Rose continues to sit, watching ragged clouds scud across a darkening sky and the busy squirrels that run amuck on the Wynfield lawn.

You rascals. It's simply not fair. You can remember hiding places for your acorns and I'm unable to remember one person. Damn, damn, damn!

A faint thud at the door startles Rose. She listens intently. Nothing. Again she wishes for Max. The sturdy Scottie is elderly, yet he alerts Rose to every footfall and barks sharply at the advent of visitors.

Maybe someone from FOOTNOTES has dropped off a book. Footnotes, my book club buddies. Certainly they don't need to remind me how far behind I am in my reading.

She opens the door to discover a small parcel wrapped in white tissue and tied with a scrap of binding twine. Rose bends slowly and carefully picks up the bundle then shuffles to her kitchen table. Her fingers explore the lumpy object beneath the soft wrapping.

Not a book, that's for sure. How exciting to get a package of any kind! The twine falls away and Rose shakes loose the tissue. A small, exquisite rabbit carved from a single block of moss-green soapstone winks up at her, ears and paws gleaming in the overhead lamp. Very slowly Rose turned it 360 degrees. It fits perfectly in her palm, the cool surface as smooth as a baby's bottom. Linear indentations between the two paws and along the ears are the only interruptions to the overall roundness. She turns it over and reads 'ACCW, Small Rabbit, 4/1/02' in a ragged scrawl.

Why, Albert Warrington! I just might cry. I am crying. What a lovely gift! I didn't even know you were a sculptor. And your timing couldn't be better. I needed something to lift my spirits! Oh, this is a treasure, and one that I shall hug close to remind me of your kindness. Why, it's a talisman of good fortune.

Rose is snuffling now, wiping her wet cheeks with a damp hanky and studying at the sculpture with moist eyes. She is enchanted with the small rabbit. Isn't a talisman supposed to protect its owner with supernatural powers? Confer a sprinkling of fairy dust? Thoughts of the mysterious Rick vanish from Rose's mind as the afternoon wanes. She happily considers the possibility of joining a sculpture class.

Should I start dabbling in sculpture? Albert doesn't have a background in the arts and look how well he's done. Ah, he knows all about bones and muscles and ligaments and body parts. Told me once he's memorized the anatomical particulars of a horse. Guess that'll be the next thing he starts sculpting, or stuffing. Brr, that gives me the willies. Stick to small animals, please, Albert! And Rose, you've just answered your own question. Stick to watercolors. You have no business dabbling in *one more thing*.

Words are easy, like the wind,
Faithful friends are hard to find.
Richard Barnfield, (1574-1627)
To his friend, Mr. R. L.

Rick Conklin wakes with a jolt, cursing himself for choosing a room at the front of the motel. 6:10 A.M. Trucks are grinding into second, then third gear as they crawl outside the SuperTen. He had slept yesterday afternoon, grabbed a bite of dinner, and then hit the sack again. He couldn't get enough sleep. The trip from Detroit seemed endless considering the number of contentious truckers who gave him rides. What normally would have taken eight, nine hours by automobile stretched into three days. Three days! Rick thinks again about of the semi-reliable, blue '72 Olds he sold to get money for this excursion. And the kid who bought it barely paid his asking price: three hundred and twenty-five dollars. All cash so he couldn't gripe. But after three days cooped up with smelly truckers who made pit stops at every watering hole along the way, he was sorry he sold it.

The one guy who picked him up in Ohio was okay. Decent fellow, older than most of the others he hitched with. Glad to have Rick along to talk to. Had a son starting college this fall. God, hate to think of how long he'll drive that rig just to pay his kid's bills. What some fathers do for their sons.

Rick lingers on this last thought.

Funny, haven't thought of my old man in years. Or Ma, either. Both of them bound to be dead by now. A permanent retirement community for sure! That's rich! Hope Dad bought the farm years ago, giving Ma a little peace in her old age. Wonder where Jason got to? Les' see, he was twelve when I left, four years younger than me. If I'm sixty, he's fifty-five or fifty-six. I should've had that librarian check on Jason when she looked up Rose. Well, first things first. I got to do what I came here to do. Then I'll head down to Colonial Beach.

Ending his reverie with a decisive grunt, Rick swings his legs over the side of the bed, stands up and stretches. He shaves and watches the grainy television and listens to the ever-grinding gears of eighteen-wheelers. After grabbing a free breakfast in the motel's lounge, he sits and scans the local paper. Someone taps him on the shoulder. He looks into the face of the desk clerk.

"You're Mr. Conklin?" he asks.

"Yeah. That's right. What of it?"

"I need to know how long you'll be staying, Mr. Conklin." He emphasizes the word 'mister' with a superior sneer on his face. "We get busy here on weekends and management needs to know if you'll still be with us on Friday and Saturday nights."

"Not if I can help it, buster," Rick replies. "I'm here on business and I plan to move on before the weekend. You go back and tell that to the management. And while you're at it, tell them that these front rooms should be half-rate. Impossible to sleep with all them trucks."

The clerk's demeanor instantly changes and he asks, "Those trucks are abominable, aren't they? I know what you mean. My room is on the front. That's why I chose night duty. Can't sleep anyway so might as well work. Gets a bit quieter in the daytime. I'll see if I can get an adjustment on your room."

"Say, thanks, pal. Didn't mean to sound off like I did. Too sleepy to make sense this morning. Lemme get another cup of coffee and I'll be in a better mood."

"Thank you, Mr. Conklin. Stop by the desk and I'll see what I can do for you."

Rick checks his watch. 9:30 in the morning and the day appears clear and promising. He returns to his room, brushes his teeth and checks his appearance in the yellowed mirror.

'Very busy on the weekends', my ass. Hell, I know how busy they get here and why. Rent these rooms by the hour. Think they'd put some decent furniture in these suites for all their important customers, as if any of 'em would notice.

Satisfied that he looks presentable in a sports shirt and his last pair of clean khakis, Rick grabs his windbreaker and leaves.

He walks a short distance up the incline and out of sight of SuperTen's night clerk. He stops on a level stretch of Route 220 and adopts a casual stance as he holds out his thumb. When a truck comes over the rise, Rick continues walking. He does not want to be dropped off at Winfield Farms from the cab of a truck.

The fifth car pauses, backs up, and the driver, a man years older than Rick, beckons him to hop in. Yep, he knows exactly where the retirement community is. Yep, happy to drop Rick near the entrance road. Yep, he is mighty glad for the company.

After riding with truckers who were either tired and taciturn or fat and foul-mouthed, Rick is shocked at hearing 'mighty glad.' He looks hard at the driver. The man's diaphragm is moving in and out with steady regular motion that causes his lower belly to push against the steering wheel like a bowling ball. Rick is fascinated, and finds his eyes fixed on the denim ball rising and falling, rising and falling. But the man doesn't wheeze and his hands are tight on the wheel. Nothing shaky about his grip.

"Name's Stroup. Sounds like *soup.* Odell Stroup. What's yours Mister?" In a gesture unexpected and sudden and with eyes never leaving the winding road, he sweeps a long right arm over to Rick and extends his hand.

Rick seizes the hand and gives it a firm grasp.

Holy mother o'... This old guy is strong! Hand feels like leather. Got to be a farmer.

"You got a real handshake mister. Tell a lot about a man the way he shakes a hand. From around these parts?" asks Stroup, leaning over to peer closely at Rick.

"Nope." Rick figures the less said the better.

"Got a name mister?"

"Name? Oh sorry. Busy thinking. Name? Yeah, Kreger. Jim Kreger."

"German, ain't it. K-r-e-g-e-r. Yep, German."

"You got it."

"New to Virginia?"

"Been here once."

Rick does not like these questions. He feels his own stomach starting to move.

"Mighty fine country here. Farmed in Eagle Rock all my life. Father before me. Bottomland, farm's right along the river. James, that is. Know the James?"

"Sorry, I don't. Say are we getting close? I don't want to miss..."

"Comin' right on it now. Time sure passes when you're having a good howdy, don't it? Here we are, Mr. Kreger. Just follow that side road, down there to the right. You'll come to them big gates in about five minutes. Old Mr. Wynfield was a humdinger, he was. Built them gates to last. Got a relative there?"

Ignoring this last question Rick climbs out and says, "Thanks Mr. Stroup. Appreciate the lift. 'Bye now."

"Odell. Odell Stroup. Everybody in these parts calls me Odell. Good luck Mister."

Rick Conklin puts his feet in the road and hoofs along towards the gates that the old humdinger built many years ago.

When tillage begins, other arts follow. The farmers therefore are the founders of human civilization.
Daniel Webster,
On Agriculture, January 13, 1840

CHAPTER
10

Jocelyn Ribble hums as she spades the earth around the slender Japanese maple. This had been a small sapling last spring and it shows promising growth. Even a slight hint of progress in this slow growing specimen cheers Jocey.

She considers the brown foliage on the daffodils. They have bloomed their last. The brownish fronds look terrible, but they are necessary for next year's blooms. She refuses to tie the foliage despite pleas from the residents who know very little about bulbs or about gardening in general, for that matter.

Well, I'll go ahead and mulch the hosta. What I need now is the fertilizer. The rhododendrons are begging for it and so are the azaleas. I better think about that before I set out any perennials. We're bound to have one more frost. Nothing's safe in Botetourt until after May 15. What is today, May 6?

Despite her yearning to plant, to start new growth, Jocey gives in to the practical, pruning, cutting back and caring for the existing *flora* and *fauna*. Jocey approaches her gardening tasks with the same single minded attention that she directs to every aspect of her life. Steady, dedicated, practical, no-nonsense Jocey. Among her siblings the cry had always been, "Leave it to Jocey. She'll know what to do–or how *to* fix it or where to go." As the youngest of the Ribble brood it was almost a given that Jocey would remain at home to look after aging parents. Wasn't she good at that? Couldn't she get some sort of garden work nearby after finishing her junior college degree? *And* live at home and nurse Mom and Pop?

So Jocey Ribble, Wynfield Farms' first (and only) professional horticulturist, labors cheerfully on a job she sees as one made in heaven—for her. Her skills with both old and new plantings are close to magical, she is a wizard at coaxing plants to live and flowers to bloom. Nothing about Jocey goes unnoticed; she is hard to miss. Nearly five feet ten with a mass of unruly dark, curly hair that always manages to escape its barrette, creamy skin and luminous gray-green eyes, the young farmer turns heads even in her trademark overalls. Her personality matches the strength of her Texas-ranger stride, open, full of good humor, quick on the uptake in every situation. The older men at Wynfield admire her talents and her figure; the older women dote on her and secretly hope she has a beau waiting in the wings.

At thirty-three, Jocey considers she has the best of all worlds— a home with parents who love and need her and a position that she adores and is good at. When one of her older sisters asked once if she "had any relationship going?" Jocey's reply had been, "No, there aren't many eligible bachelors at Wynfield Farms." Home and work were her life. Until this morning.

She does not see the stranger sitting on the bench until she rounds the corner to give the dianthus a sprinkling of lime.

"I've been watching you," he tosses out casually.

"Me?"

"Yeah, for the past half-hour or so. You're a fast worker. Look like you enjoy what you do." Rick has been resting on the inviting bench after his hike from the main road. It was more of a trek than his friend from Eagle Rock had indicated.

Jocey scowls at the man. What is he doing out here? Why is he in no hurry to leave? He's too young to be a resident at Wynfield. Someone's brother? Son? Interviewing for a job? She knows of no openings.

"Something I can help you with, Mister?" Jocey asks finally.

Rick stands and walks closer to Jocey. "I'm sort of look-ing for an old acquaintance. Someone you might know if you've been working here a while."

"I've been at Wynfield Farms from the beginning. Who is it?"

"Rose Mason. I mean, Rose *McNess*. Know the lady?"

Jocey's expression softens and her smile broadens, "Oh, she's my favorite resident. Of course I know Mrs. McNess. Everyone does. She's great. Only not too great at this point, I'm afraid."

Rick's jaw drops, Oh my God, don't tell me she's kicked the bucket. All this way and Rose dead before he could even see her...

"What's the matter? Didn't die, I hope?"

Jocey giggles. "No, no, nothing that awful. She fell, a little over a month ago, right over there." She points to the bridge. "She broke her hip, then had to have a hip replace-ment, so she's sort of laid up right now. Knowing Mrs. McNess, it won't keep her down for long."

"Is she in the hospital?" Rick asks, almost afraid to hear the reply.

"Heavens, no! They hardly keep you for a week these days, unless you've had brain surgery. Mrs. McNess is up and about on a walker. But she's not up to seeing many visitors. Stays mostly in her room, I believe."

"That's too bad. I'm passing through and I'd hoped to see her again. Very *much* hoped to see her."

"I'll be happy to give her a message from you, Mr...." offers Jocey, noticing for the first time how tall the man is and how the gray in his thick hair make him look, well, al-most distinguished. Except for those fingernails. Grimy cu-ticles. Someone should tell him about cleaning his nails.

"Oh, no, that won't be necessary. I'll try back in a few days. She's pretty popular, huh?"

Rick has already mailed two letters to Rose. Now he wants to contact her personally, to surprise her and see her expression when he shows up. Would she still have that scattershot of freckles across her nose? Would her hair be graying as his was doing?

"Mrs. McNess is the most popular person at Wynfield Farms. She hasn't been here all that long, but she gets things moving. When did you know her?" Jocey is genuinely curious about this man. She wouldn't call him Rose McNess's type, even though he is attractive. Perhaps a business friend of her husband's, or one of her husbands. Rose had, after all, been married twice, or so Jocey had heard from one of the other residents.

"Say," says the stranger, "I didn't answer your question. I'm Rick. Rick Conklin. And you are...?"

"Jocelyn Ribble. I'm the horticulturist."

"*Miss* Ribble, I take it?" Rick saw no rings on Jocey's left hand when she took off her gloves to wipe her forehead, now smudged with Montremont soil.

"Yes, of course, *Miss* Ribble."

"That's two of us. I'm not married. Say, I've got a swell idea. Can I treat you to lunch? I don't know this area very well but I do know it's getting on toward lunchtime and if you're willing, I'd like to take you to eat."

It may have been smudge on her forehead or the way her curls drifted over her left eye that causes Rick's heart to flip-flop. He is smitten with Jocey Ribble.

Jocey blushes at the unexpected offer. What should I say? I barely know this man's name. Rick something or other. But he's a friend of Mrs. McNess, and that counts for a lot in my book. She wouldn't tolerate just anybody. Lunch, munch. Did I tell Mom I'd be home? I don't think so. They were driving into Roanoke to see Dad's doctor. Should I say yes? Where would we go? Fincastle, I guess. Well, why not?

"I *suppose* I could do lunch. That would be a nice change. If you don't mind my overalls. This is my uniform." Jocey smiles at Rick with the expression of a winsome child.

She's pretty as a picture, and sexy as hell, Rick concludes. An apple ripe for the picking. "There's just one hitch, Jocey. My car's back at the place in Daleville. Transmission's shot. You don't happen to have wheels, do you?" Rick hopes he sounds sincere; if not, the whole deal is off.

"How'd you get out here?" asks Jocey.

"Taxi. Big bucks, but it's worth it."

"Well, of course I've got a car. Rather, a truck. If you don't mind riding in a truck."

"I'm used to trucks. That'd be great if you don't mind. Besides, you'll have to tell me where to go anyway. I don't know this area."

"Okay. Come on down to the greenhouse with me while I put the tools away. My truck is in the lot behind the greenhouse. It won't take a minute."

"Would you mind if I wait here? This view is so spectacular I'd like to sit and stare a little longer." Rick is surprised at the spontaneity—he hopes—of his rejoinder. He does not want to risk Rose seeing him yet. No, he wants a personal and surprise encounter. Fate has a way of playing tricks. Rose Mason might spot him if he went near the big house.

"Suit yourself. Give me ten minutes and I'll pick you up on the driveway." Jocey gestures toward the main drive, smiles, and sets off with her tools and baskets toward the greenhouse.

At that moment Chef Leon glances out the Wynfield kitchen window and sees Jocey coming down the hill from the gardens. Three years I've been trying to court that woman and nothing! Always happy to see me but nothing else. Not even a date! Of course, part of it's my fault. Only been free of Lorraine for a year, but Jocey won't let me get close. Why does she look so happy now? She goes home at lunchtime. Maybe she's had good news about her dad's health. *C'est la vie.* With that, Chef Leon dismisses pretty, smiling Jocey from his mind and turns to the Cobb salad he is preparing for forty-two lunch regulars.

Jocelyn Ribble Prepares For Her First (True) Date

Oh God, what have I gotten into? Did I really tell Rose's friend I would go to lunch with him? Stupid question, Jocey, you sure did or you wouldn't be hustling back to the greenhouse to primp. This is a date, Jocey, not a chance meeting. Lunch. That's all. I'm not marryin' the guy, just going to lunch. So why am I so nervous? Never done this, that's why. Gone off with someone for lunch, that is. Leon doesn't count. I always eat in the kitchen with him and the staff. Well, I'll do the best I can. Where's the lip gloss? Hairbrush? Not much I can do to tame the hair. And he is nice in a foreign looking sort of way. Definitely not from around here. Wish he had cleaner fingernails. Listen to me, *picky, picky, picky.*

J ocey drives. This makes sense, her truck, her territory, with a stranger sitting beside her on the front seat. And he *is* a stranger. Didn't they just meet an hour ago and didn't she agree to lunch? Is that why she feels queasy, a little jittery, and is talking a mile a minute? She has been chattering away nonstop since her passenger climbed into the truck. The sun bouncing off the chrome trim causes Jocey to blink and pause in her string of words. She is slightly giddy. This is her first real date, if lunch at the local diner with a total stranger is a real date.

"...so my spring and summer schedules are pretty much the same each year. We don't get too many dramatic weather changes out here. How about you? Where you from?"

"Midwest. Recently, Detroit. Or as you say in the south, Deee-troit."

"I *don't* say that and I'm from the south," she says petulantly. "Here we are, Fincastle's finest."

"Whatdidya call this town?" Rick asks as Jocey expertly backs her truck into a space beside the token-white-washed anchor at the edge of the *Skipperjack's* parking lot.

"Fincastle. It is one of the oldest pre-Revolutionary towns in the Shenandoah Valley."

"One of those fake towns? Where's the river? Got an anchor, got to be a river."

"It is not a fake. But there is no river. No river, no lake, not even a pond. Just good seafood."

"Just kidding about the fake part, Jocelyn. I used to work in a fake town, up in Michigan. It was made to look old timey, but it was phony from the git-go. And tourists loved it. You say this is the real thing?"

Rick follows Jocey from the truck into the restaurant where he guides her to a booth on the shady side of the dining area.

He's not hard to talk to, only I can't tell when he's kidding or being serious. Fake town my foot! I should give him a history lesson right now. I could tell him a few things about Fincastle, that's for sure. Jocey scans the room. Good. Lunch crowd's gone. No one I know in here today.

Rick grabs the large laminated menus crammed between the sugar bowl and napkin holder. They both frown and read the menu with as much intensity as if it held the hottest tips from the day's stock market. A bored waitress appears. Pad and pencil in hand, she is eager to take their orders so she can finish her shift.

Rick answers her "Whatillitbe?" with "Two beers, please. Corona, extra lime."

"Oh, I don't know," begins Jocey.

Over her protests, Rick promises that a cup of coffee will right any wrong before she returns to work.

Only I got other plans for this little lady. I don't think she's going to go back to work this afternoon. Like I said, an apple ripe for the picking.

They both order the fried shrimp /slaw/hush puppy combo. ("Best thing on the menu," offers the waitress) and when their meals arrive they settle into serious eating. Jocey concentrates on spearing her shrimp and dividing one hush puppy into two. The beer is icy cold. She starts to relax, looks at Rick, and asks him about himself.

She is a willing audience as he talks about his early years in South Dakota and his carnival adventures, his engineering work in Detroit, and the fake town he knows. Then he regales her about his new job as a lifeguard at Colonial Beach. Jocey is speechless. And impressed.

"But... you're too..." she stammers.

"Old. I know what you're thinking. Too old. Not on your life young lady. I can bench press 200 pounds. Easy. I'm in good shape to rescue any damsel in distress."

"Wow."

"Wanna know of some of the things the Red Cross makes you practice before you hit the beach?" he asks.

"I guess," Jocey replies, nervously fingering at her watch.

"First you got to be able to swim at least 100 yards, and then you got to practice dragging a rescue tube behind your behind. Then you learn the CPR techniques, you know, getting the water out of person who swallowed too much and making sure their heart beats strong again. And all the first aid treatments from bee stings to broken backs."

"And you can do all that? I mean, you've been trained to do those things?"

"Oh sure, Miss Joc-e-lyn Ribble. I told you I've done lots of things. Life guarding was one of 'em. That's why they want me again."

Lunch stretches on, and by two-thirty in the afternoon Jocey is pleasantly sleepy and protests to Rick Conklin that really, she should be getting back to work. Could she drop him anyplace?

One other couple is still eating a late lunch at the *Skipperjack*. Their table is in the far corner and the man has just dropped several quarters in the vintage jukebox. George Jones's "He Stopped Loving Her Today" starts wailing to the near empty restaurant.

"Oh not yet, Jocey. We got to dance to *this*. C'mon. This is a classic. 'Bout the greatest country song ever written, that's all. Ol' Possom, George Jones himself. What'ya afraid of, little lady?"

"I told you I've really got to be getting back. Besides, I haven't danced in years." But she had *wanted* to dance all those years, and she did now, this afternoon, with a man nearly twice her age and with nothing but trouble on his mind. He presses her close to him and nuzzles in her hair. She feels herself getting hot and full of new, bewildering feelings. He is hard, and she feels him through her overalls. The dancing, stumbling lightheaded to her truck, handing him the keys so he could drive her back to Wynfield, shortcutting to a secluded cul-de-sac on a back road out of Fincastle, heavy petting with his grimy hands grabbing at her breasts—it is all a terrible mistake. Jocey realizes this the minute the second beer begins to wear off. Alarm and fear take over.

This is all wrong! Who is this man? What am I doing here? Got to get away, got to make him stop. Stop, NOW! "Stop it, Rick Conklin! Stop it, I say. I'm not the kind of girl you took me for. I know every policeman on the road and I'll have you strung up in no time if you don't let me go. Now." Jocey backs away from Rick, crouching against the passenger's door. Those steely blue eyes. I think I've put some shame in them.

She is in full control of her senses once again and furious, not only with herself but with this man. "And give me my keys. I'll drop you in Daleville as payment for my lunch. I *should* leave you out here in the woods."

Rick knows he has met his match. Jocey's brown eyes gleam: her mouth forms into a thin, hard line of determination. He sheepishly hands over the keys and walks around the front of the truck to trade seats.

"I'm sorry, Jocey. *Really.* Must've been the beer. I don't usually drink in the middle of the day. I would never do anything to hurt you, believe me."

"Oh, shut up. You almost did," Jocey spits through clenched teeth.

Jocey drops Rick Conklin at the Mobil station in Daleville and drives slowly home. It is nearly five in the afternoon. Early, her normal workdays run until six or six-thirty. She parks at the back of the Ribble's modest bungalow and rests her head on the steering wheel.

What have I done? Or nearly done? What can I tell Mom? Her stomach hurts. Nauseous with beer and memory of the long afternoon, she hurts all over.

"I'm home because I'm feeling sick, Ma," she calls to her parents. "I'm going up to bed."

Rick Conklin Considers His Luncheon Date With Jocelyn Ribble

What a tease! Hot little prissy-britches, beggin' for some lovin' but just couldn't let herself go. Damn! Hope this date didn't blow my chances with Rose. Nah—I'll get back to Wynfield Farms early tomorrow mornin' and surprise Rose, just like I planned. Miss Joc-e-lyn Ribble won't have time to get to Rose before I do. Besides, *she* asked for it; I wasn't leading her on or anything. Think Ol' Possum done it. She loved that dancin' close. Nah, wipe this date off your slate, Rick. Zero. Rose is the class-act and the Class Act is what I am here to catch.

CHAPTER

12

Rose enters her apartment and shuffles slowly to her favorite wing chair where she collapses, exhausted by the activities of the past six hours. They have seemed interminable.

This is the day of anticipated visit by the Japanese sociologists. Mrs. Gallentine's organizational plans are worthy of an invasion of the whole of Europe. Every Wynfield staff member has his or her specific assignments and a cadre of residents volunteered as tour guides for the day. Rose agrees to an abbreviated shift and that on the heels of her therapy with Inge. All the planning reaped great dividends. The visitors enjoyed a highly successful day at a premier retirement community. The tours were appreciated and the luncheon was arguably one of the best meals Chef Leon had ever attempted. Mrs. Gallentine, Rose is convinced, is smiling like the Cheshire Cat.

The only glitch in the day was a no-show by Jocey Ribble. Early this morning she had called in sick. At the eleventh hour Mrs. G. had drafted Rose, Ellie and Frances to pinch-hit as florists.

"Thank heavens for Frances," Rose sighs, remembering how her garden–club pal had commandeered the shears and pulled the orchid and fern creations together for twenty tables. "And they did look lovely. Our new friends were impressed. What a shame Jocey had to miss hearing all the nice things they had to say about her work."

Rose's physical self now assumes command of her psyche self and shuts down her tired body for a deep slumber. The faded wing chair embraces its occupant with arms of pure down. The ring of the telephone jars Rose to a wakeful state. It is half-past six in the evening.

Drat. Why didn't I take that instrument off the hook? Coming, coming, she complains, fuzzy with sleep as she hobbles to the kitchen.

Mrs. Gallentine is on the line. Could Mrs. McNess spare a moment? Of course. Rose listens to the lengthy account of the visitors' highly favorable impressions of Wynfield Farms. A pause, and the Resident Director drops her bombshell. One of the Japanese visitors had fallen asleep in the garden and is now stranded indefinitely at Wynfield Farms. Tour leader, ticket, topcoat, trunk, all were *en route* to Japan. Another pause. Would Mrs. McNess be up to coming to her office to chat with the poor fellow while Mrs. Gallentine telephoned the authorities?

A few aspects of Wynfield Farms Retirement Community
that the Visiting Japanese Sociologists Found Memorable

Living and working arrangement of home "Incredible! Everyone has own space for living, shared areas for work and social activities. Most gracious arrangement."

Mrs. Paula Gallentine "A tall black Goddess commands an Army!"

Montremont Gardens "Nature in harmony with earth, water and sky."

Mrs. McNess "A lively woman despite infirm leg."

Mrs. Johnson "Call me 'Ellie'? Are all Americans this informal?"

Mrs. Keynes-Johnson "Ah, the lady with the lichens."

Mr. Everett "A true scholar—*summa est.*"

Food "So delicious. Our special rice, Kymo crackers, fresh crab, such delicacies we have not have since leaving home three weeks ago. All elegant preparation and work of one man!"

Floral centerpieces "Ah! Works of art! Delicate as the master's touch: ferns and orchids kissed by the Butterfly. But where is the young designer who dared create such beauty for us?"

13

Rose restores the telephone to its bracket and leans against the kitchen wall. She is stunned and too tired to move.

What next? I am tired and my hip aches and it's half past six. But I can't refuse Mrs. Gallentine. She has to be weary also, planning for this group and entertaining them royally all afternoon. And now a left over with no place to go. If that doesn't beat all. How could a grown man simply go to sleep and let the tour roar off without him? I better get myself together and go down to the office. Mrs. Gallentine sounded desperate. I guess I'm the only resident at Wynfield Farms with a tangible Japanese connection.

Damnation. Why did I ever think I was going to work at the computer today? Not going to kid myself that I'll feel like it when I return. Might as well stay down and eat dinner. Lunch was a long time ago.

A fresh blouse, a powder-blue cardigan, lipstick and a quick brush of her hair and Rose looks less bedraggled. There, best I can manage.

She is shutting the apartment door when Ellie Johnson comes into view down the hallway.

"Rose wait! I must show you my bargain of the day!"

Ellie is breathless, and Rose asks, "What have you found now Ellie? After all your London treasures last year nothing you buy would surprise me."

"Look!" she crows triumphantly. "Six bucks on the throw-away table at Wal-Mart." She lifts her right foot and points happily to the ugliest shoe Rose has ever seen. Ellie's new shoes are multi-strapped sandals on 3-inch platform soles in a color that can only be described as Pepto-Bismol pink.

"What can I say, Ellie?" Rose laughs, "Except they are unique. Are you sure the shoe fits?"

"Most comfortable shoes I've ever had on my feet. At six bucks, what could I lose? Imagine the nerve—putting these on the throwaway table. Where are *you* off to, if I may inquire?"

"Mrs. Gallentine had a surprise find too, Ellie. Not a throwaway but a stowaway. One of the Japanese fell asleep in our gardens and missed the bus. He may be stranded here *indefinitely* and Mrs. Gallentine asked me to come down and talk with him. I think she's tearing her hair out at this point."

"Oh God, Rose, and I've stopped you for a fashion show. But there's something else. Come in, just for a sec. I must show you the latest."

"Ellie, I really must go," Rose protests. She reluctantly enters Ellie's apartment and watches as her friend retrieves a brown lunch bag from beneath the cushions on her over-size couch.

"Look!" She empties the contents into her hands and brandishes them in front of Rose.

"What in the world? Firecrackers? Am I right? Old-fashioned Fourth of July firecrackers? Ellie where did you...?"

"Nothing *but* firecrackers. I found these little beauties in the hallway as I was dashing for the bus. The bag was crumpled and open and I stopped to pick it up. I thought it was just trash, then these fell out. Six of them. I was so shocked I dashed back and pushed the bag beneath the pillows. Missed the damn bus into town, incidentally."

"Ellie do you think this is a prank? Are we being set up?"

"I think someone has a serious problem. Should I report this?"

"Oh, heavens, Ellie, not now, while the stowaway problem is paramount. Let's put our heads together tonight."

"You're right, Rose, as usual. This might be more than even the unflappable Mrs. G. could take at this point. I do think it's related to the trash fires though. Don't you?"

"Absolutely," agrees Rose. "Now I simply must get down to the office—"

"If you decide to stay down for dinner save me a chair. And thanks for approving my shoes."

Ellie sees Rose to the door and waves goodbye.

Rose patiently makes her way to Mrs. Gallentine's office. The stowaway, a polite, very bewildered, small sad-faced man with huge brown eyes, sits quietly lost in a large leather chair.

"Professor Yokamura from Tokyo, this is Mrs. Rose McNess of Wynfield Farms." Jubilant with relief at seeing Rose, Mrs. Gallentine continues, "Mrs. McNess has family in Japan at present. I'm sure you two will have much to talk about while I try to locate your group. Mrs. McNess, would you please escort Professor Yokamura to someplace more comfortable?"

"We'll have lots to talk about Mrs. G. I think the pub is the perfect spot. Our friend may need something to bolster his spirits after this experience. Shall we go Professor Yokamura?"

Rose leads the way to *The Rose and The Grape* and indicates a corner table. If the visitor is embarrassed at having slept through the bus's departure, he does not show it. Mrs. Gallentine has assured him of accommodations in one of the guest rooms and he confesses to Rose that he is looking forward to being the lone Japanese citizen in Wynfield Farms for the evening.

He prefers single malt Scotch, a fact that endears him to Rose immediately. She asks the barmaid to bring the professor a drink of Wynfield's finest, plain tonic for herself, then settles down to learn about her newest best friend.

"I am interested in what you just said, Professor, about being the only Japanese in Wynfield Farms. You don't miss your traveling companions?"

"In our country, Mrs. McNess, we have little opportunity to be alone. In everything we do, we are with fellow man. I teach at a large university, and since my beloved wife's death two years ago, I share two rooms with another professor. Faculty has two hundred teachers and I am professor to three hundred students. Very little time to be alone."

Rose is intrigued by Professor Yokamura's poignant confession. She commends him on his command of the English language and shares with him her penchant for being alone also.

"Here in the United States, Professor, too many people live alone, either by choice or by chance. Sometimes the situations, especially for the elderly, can be tragic. I've had a life of togetherness, so, as you, I appreciate solitude. This is why places like Wynfield Farms are healthy. In a community, people always look out for one another but do not suffocate them. Do I make sense, Professor Yokamura?"

"Ah, Mrs. McNess. I can tell you are a wise woman. That is why our group is studying these retirement towns. Asians are very proud and insist on taking care of their own. Old parents are expected to live in small houses already crowded with adolescents and working parents. They may be neglected and sometimes there is tragedy. By examining many places as Wynfield, our group hopes to make recommendations to Japanese government. We may start to build communities for some of our elderly."

"I hope the group's visit to Wynfield Farms was favorable, Professor. I know yours will be, because of this bonus time. Do you think they were impressed with what we showed them?"

"I shall send you full report, Mrs. McNess. Please, would you now tell me about your family in Japan?"

The next hour passes quickly as questions fly back and forth. They are almost sorry when Mrs. Gallentine arrives and announces that she'd secured a ticket for the professor for Thursday morning. Until then, Father Charlie has volunteered to find him extra clothing and toiletry articles.

"Father Charlie is saving a table for four in the dining room, Mrs. McNess. I knew you'd probably want Mrs. Johnson to join you, and I thought four people would ensure quiet conversation time with the professor this evening. Any objections?"

"Perfect, Mrs. Gallentine. The professor and I have had a delightful time getting acquainted. Father Charlie and Ellie will be equally enchanted with our guest."

At the evening's conclusion, Professor Yokamura bowed politely to his new friends and allowed Father Charlie to shepherd him to the guest quarters for the night.

"What a gentleman," says Ellie. "He's so interesting. His porcelains must be world class. Did you hear that bit about a museum in Tokyo wanting every piece for its permanent collection?"

"I did," replies Rose. "And the professor is not given to boasting. Almost too modest and self-effacing. I'll bet he enjoys his two nights here at Wynfield Farms. He'll even have a room to himself. He can wander around and be himself without hordes of people. All the luxuries we take for granted in our old age. Creature comforts, Ellie, creature comforts."

"I hate to raise an unpleasant subject again, Rose, but have you had a chance to think about the matter I sprang on you this afternoon? As in *bang bang*?"

"Gosh, no Ellie. With the professor and then dinner, I surely haven't. Have *you* had any more thoughts? Or clues?"

"Not yet. I'm racking my feeble brain. Perhaps they're meant to be party favors for a birthday party. But I can't begin to think who has a birthday coming up."

"Did you hide the package in a safe place?"

"You bet. Put it in Vincent's cage, under the night wraps. Gosh, I miss that little bird. And I've also made careful notes about where I found the bag of stuff and when Mrs. G. found the collections she's reported. I'm keeping a journal, Rose. I don't like it. It's almost as if we were under siege."

"Now, Ellie, it's not quite that bad. I'll put my mind on

it tomorrow but tonight I'm just too tired to think anymore. Come on, let's go upstairs."

When Rose finally lowers herself into bed, she allows herself a giggle and murmurs, "I, too, am a creature definitely in need of comfort. Our professor is not alone in his earthly desires."

Ellie Johnson Scribbles Furiously in her Journal

"Write it bold and Write it in GOLD!" That is exactly what I am going to do. Matches, charred rags and now FIRECRACKERS! Someone is either nuts or going on a rampage and trying to burn us all to cinders. Right in our beds, right here at Wynfield farms. I don't think Rose is taking this as seriously as I am. She's preoccupied with the professor and her mystery man. But I found the evidence and may be the target of the next attack—Night vision goggles! They make them in Roanoke—why can't I purchase a pair then stalk the halls in the wee hours to find out who is dropping these curious clues?

14

Inge suggests cutting Rose's therapy session short today. "You're trying *too* hard, Mrs. McNess. You can make that new hip do just so much and no more. You're my star pupil and I would hate to see you regress now. Let's call it quits this morning. I think you overdid it yesterday. Tie a big bow on that walker if it annoys you so much. The cane is coming next week, I promise."

Rose feels like a naughty child suspended from school. Well, maybe I did overdo a bit yesterday. I know I wasn't concentrating this morning; I was thinking of firecrackers and matchbooks and the professor. Wonder what he is up to? Reading, perhaps, unless Ellie took him shopping. She did threaten that at dinner. Rose smiles at the thought of Ellie and the professor at Wal-Mart or the mall.

She makes her way to the reception hall and the familiar chair that always welcomes her. She flexes the fingers on both hands and wonders whether the strain she feels is merely arthritis or stress from gripping her walker. She is examining her left hand when a shadow falls across her lap. She looks up to see a tall man with dark hair and a wide smile that accentuates the deep cleft in his chin. His steel blue eyes pin Rose to her chair.

"Hello, Rose Mason."

Rose blanches. Half expecting Professor Yokamura, she

is startled by a stranger addressing her by her maiden name. She has not been Rose Mason in over forty years. "I-I'm sorry. I don't seem to be able to place you. *Should* I know you?" Despite the safety of her surroundings, Rose is powerless to prevent the unsettling feelings that now engulf her.

"Rick. Rick Conklin. Oh yes, you did know me, a long time ago. But what is this? Did you fall?" His tone is jocular, confident. Jocey had told Rick all about Rose's accident, but he hopes inquiring about the obvious may hide his own momentary nervousness.

Damn if I didn't get lucky. Rose sitting right here in the middle of this big empty room. She's as pretty as ever. Gotta go slow, don't want to tip my hand right away.

"Your guess is correct." Rose overcomes her squeamishness and says "You say I *did* know you?"

He certainly is a nice looking man! That cleft in his chin is so pronounced it almost chisels the chin in half. What a sweet smile, almost boyish. He must be in his late fifties; prematurely gray hair? No, this fellow is older than he appears. Broad shoulders. Neatly dressed, well pressed shirt and trousers. Rose's mind is racing.

"Is there somewhere we can talk? This place is an auditorium. Ceiling's so high I can hear echoes. Gives me the creeps."

Mrs. Gallentine and Miss Mueller happen to choose this moment to emerge from the Director's office. Mrs. Gallentine inspects Rose's caller with a withering stare.

"How are you feeling this morning, Mrs. McNess? I shoved a lot of responsibility on you yesterday. But I'm so grateful for all you did for the professor." Mrs. Gallentine's smile is genuine and directed solely to Rose.

"Pshaw! Think nothing of it. I may have overdone a bit, but all for a good cause. I feel fine. I'll talk with you later. I am about to show my friend the pub"

"I'm happy to see you up and around again," calls the young receptionist as she leaves with Mrs. Gallentine. She smiles ingenuously, a smile, Rose notes, aimed toward Rick.

"Pub?" asks Rick. "Should we drive, Rose?"

Rose wants to scream, "Stop calling me Rose!" I can't even remember your name and I certainly wasn't going to ask you in front of Mrs. Gallentine and that—that child. They'd really think I was losing my marbles.

"No, no," Rose says with a laugh, "follow me. This is our favorite gathering place. One can order coffee, soft drinks, and of course, regular pub fare. And it is much more pleasant than being out here in the reception area."

Rick follows Rose into *The Rose and The Grape*.

"Hey, I'm impressed. Snazzy. Named for you by any chance?"

"As a matter of fact, it is," Rose admits. "Here, have a seat while I spoon myself into the chair." Rose points to a table and looks around. Bob Lesley and Albert Warrington are seated in a corner booth drinking coffee and working crossword puzzles. A forlorn Bob Jenkins reads his newspaper nearby. Rose waves vaguely to acknowledge their quizzical expressions. Then she remembers the rabbit and calls softly, "Albert—until you're properly thanked, I adore my sculpture." He grins in acknowledgement and returns to his puzzle.

"Now, before we order, I must ask you to tell me your name once again. I hate to be rude but I have no inkling of who you are. Yet you know my maiden name—"

"Rick Conklin, Virginia Beach, 1961. July, 1961. Didn't you get my letters?"

The letters. Of course. Rose's world as she knows it shifts in that instant. Her brain freezes, as it had so many years ago when she witnessed a tragedy. She cannot verbalize or reconstruct a moment of the event that traumatized her. The only thing she remembers is the date, July, 1961.

The man continues gently, "We had a swell time together, you and I. You bragged about being a champion swimmer and gave me tips on being a better lifeguard. I was a lifeguard in Virginia Beach that summer."

"Would you—would you mind getting us a cup of coffee, Dick? Your name . . . it is Dick, isn't it?"

"*Rick. Rick Conklin.* Sure. I'll be glad to get it. Still take it black?"

How does he know how I like my coffee? "Black. Black and hot, please."

Virginia Beach, 1961. I was there. Who is this Rick Conklin? That was after college, after Europe. But how did I get to Virginia Beach? Who did I know? Surely I wouldn't have gone by myself. Oh, why can't I remember whatever it is that is circling around in my mind? Panic replaces the former unsettled thoughts.

"Here we are. I take mine black, too, Rose. We drank lots of coffee back then, mostly at Dot's. Does that ring a bell?"

"No, I'm afraid not. I'm sorry, Rick. I just cannot place you. My life has been a full one. I've been married and widowed twice, and moved more times than I care to count. My memory is like the boxes I've shifted from move to move. I discard a few and keep the favorites. I like the good memories. I'm touched that you remember me and took the trouble to look me up. How did you find 'Rose Mason' after all these years?"

"Easy. The Internet."

"You're a computer expert?"

"Not really. But when I set my mind to something, I go for it. And I had my mind, and heart, set on finding you."

Rose ignores this. "But your accent. It's not a Southern accent. Where are you from? And what brought you to Virginia? Surely you're not going to tell me you came all the way to Fincastle, Virginia to look up Rose Mason?"

"Yep. That's it, exactly."

"But how did you know I'd even be alive or the Rose Mason you knew?"

"I was willing to chance it and I confess to having another reason to come. You may not believe this, but I am returning to work as a lifeguard again. After forty years. What d'ya think of that?" Unconsciously Rick has slipped into his Detroit slang. He is feeling comfortable with himself by this time; mentioning his new job bolsters his cocky attitude.

"A lifeguard? But you're, you're—"

"Too old? I've heard that before! Nah, they advertised, I applied, and they even paid my way down here to the Old Dominion. Colonial Beach is a short hop away, so I thought I'd circle by here first and see if we . . . well, if we could renew our friendship before I renewed my lifeguard skills. Have to report to Colonial Beach for a final interview next week. They're desperate for experienced lifeguards on Virginia's beaches. Teenagers don't want to work anymore. Think the pay's too low."

"What a coincidence. Some friends of mine were talking about that very thing just the other day. They had read an article in the paper."

"Yeah. That's how I first heard about the vacancies. *Roanoke Times*, it was."

That's why I've been hanging around that sleazy motel. Used up most of my advance, even with hitching rides to get here. Jeeze, Rose, your memory don't kick in soon, I'm outta here, Rick thinks.

"You say you report next week?"

Oh Lord, what should I do? Common sense tells me to say goodbye Rick and good riddance. The other side of me says invite him to stay, try to uncover the past and remember what he meant in my life. I better say something quick. This coffee is cold and I don't wish to linger over another cup.

"Rick," Rose says evenly, "I am racking my brain to place you. I hope you aren't insulted. It's just that...well, I haven't been myself after this fall, and my mind plays tricks on me. I get fuzzy and forget all sorts of things. I lose my keys and misplace my glasses. I told you I've discarded boxes of memories. I am, you must understand, an old woman."

"Oh no, Rose, that's not true. I was twenty and you were thirty-three in 1961. I know exactly how old you are. And you ain't old!"

Rose is both flattered and flustered. She is reluctant to ask the next question but she knows she must. She whispers, "I hesitate to ask, Rick, but tell me truthfully, did we have a romantic, ah, feeling for each other that summer?"

In a low voice he replies, "Rose, you really don't remember?"

Rick is crestfallen but his face reveals nothing. Sitting
across from Rose Mason, now McNess, he thinks she is even
more beautiful than forty years ago. Her skin is clear, a few
lines where lines are supposed to be. The wispy curls that
frame her small face have gray in them, but no more than he
has. Her gaze is steady and intelligent, just as he remembered. His heart beats so loudly he is sure Rose can hear it
above the clink of the spoon he is fiddling with.

"I'm sorry, Rick. I guess you think I had flings at all
the beaches. A real flirt. I assure you I did *not*. I married in
the fall of 1961. That is so distant, so long ago...but I'll tell
you what."

One glance at Rick's stricken look and Rose's benevo-
lence overcomes her fears. I feel terrible! Rick Conklin has
come all the way to Virginia to find me and I cannot remember him. Did he say where he came from? I better get that
straight. The very least I can do is invite him to dinner. No
need to delve into the past, romance or no romance. I'll say
he is a friend from after the war or after college, after anything. Which is the truth. We'll have dinner and I'll find out
what really happened that July. Then I can wave goodbye to
him forever.

"I interrupted myself Rick. Why don't you join me for
dinner tomorrow evening? The Wynfield Dining Room is quite
elegant and the meals superb. Will you be my guest?"

"Only if I may bring a bottle of bubbly as my contribution."

"That's thoughtful of you, but wine is included with
dinner if we desire. We live very well here at Wynfield Farms."

"Swell. May I come for you in your apartment, Rose?
I'd like to see where you live, look at pictures of your family.
Sort of get an idea of how you're getting along."

"Lovely. Plan on about six and we'll have a drink before dinner. My apartment is 208. Just stop at the Reception
Desk, where we met, and tell Miss Mueller you're my guest.

Take the elevator on the left. I'm sorry I can't offer you a guided tour of Wynfield Farms. But you've given me something to look forward to tomorrow evening."

Sure as hell hope so. Another night to wait here. Rose looks blank as a slate. She is clueless about that day on the beach, as well as who I am. Why should she forgive me if she can't remember who I am to forgive? Should I just hit her for some money and get out of town? Doesn't look like she has any money. No memory, no money. Really know how to pick 'em, Rick.

"And I'll look forward to it, too, Rose. I still remember your favorite food."

"You *do?*"

"Crab cakes with a wedge of fresh lemon. And hold the mayo. Dot really knew how to make those crab cakes. Man, were they good!"

RICK CONKLIN ANALYZES HIS STATUS
AT WYNFIELD FARMS

O, man! Rose Mason, I mean *McNess,* is still as beautiful as ever. Why didn't I try to find her after all that mess? Why didn't...hell ... no use even thinking that. Enjoy the moment Rick. She's nice as ever, sweet, still classy, still smart. God, the stares of those old gents in the pub. Thought they were going to eat me alive. Guess they are Rose's watchdogs; certainly gave me the old once-over. What did they think I was going to do, throw her over my shoulder and run? Sure made me feel young. They must be 80, 90 years old if they're a day. But Rose don't seem any older than back in '61. Wonder if she has any idea how different our lives have been since we met at the beach?

15

Bob Lesley and Albert Warrington observe Rose and her companion as they walked slowly from *The Rose and The Grape*. Neither of the two men spoke for some time. Bob Jenkins was also a spectator, having finished the newspaper some minutes before.

"As a physician, I submit that our Rose is making re-markable progress. Just proves what I always say, attitude is key to recovery from any setback, physical or mental." Bob Lesley rubs his chin thoughtfully as he speaks.

"I agree with you, Bob, even with my feeble knowledge of anatomy," concurs Albert Warrington.

"Feeble! Don't be so self-deprecating, my friend. With all the taxidermy you meddle with, you probably know more about bones and joints than most orthopedic surgeons."

"Where is Professor Yokamura this morning? Seen him today?"

"I gather he's being called 'Taki' now, especially by the ladies. No, haven't seen him yet. Fine man. Perhaps he's out meditating, on his own for a while," says Bob Lesley.

"Do you think having a Japanese citizen here engen-ders any animosity from our veterans?" asks Albert Warrington.

"Possibly at first, just hearing 'Japanese citizen'. But as Father Charlie says, he's a human being, and we can't lay the blame for the entire aggression on one individual's shoulders. The professor represents such fine morals and civility that he is almost a walking apology for the nation's actions." It is obvious that the good doctor has given thought to Albert's question.

The two friends enjoy a quiet chuckle, rehashing the ludicrous scenario of discovering the sleeping professor in the garden.

"Mind if I join you?" asks Bob Jenkins, paper in hand.

"Please do," Bob Lesley replies jovially. "Bring your chair over and we'll have a second cup of coffee together. And perhaps a sandwich. How's the wife Bob? Better today?"

"Esther's about the same. Health care worker's with her now. I can't stay for a sandwich but I will have coffee. I couldn't help overhearing your comments about Rose. Darn shame about her fall. She should have reduced her hazards on that path. You both know my feelings on that particular subject. Glad to have her walking the halls again, even on a walker. But it's not her recovery I'm worried about."

Bob and Albert stare dumbly at their friend.

"I know what you're about to say, Bob," intones Albert. "You're about to put into words what the doctor and I are reluctant to say."

"That man looks as if he is up to no good," growls Bob Jenkins. "Rose McNess has the kindest heart in this place and I think she's being taken. What's your theory, Doc?"

"I admit I didn't like his familiarity with our Rose, leaning in close for cozy conversation. He's certainly no professional. The guy acted more like a young buck than an over-the-hill senior."

Albert Warrington considers the doctor's response. "I agree he was a bit intimate in his conversational style but he didn't make egregious gestures or take any liberties with Rose. As a matter of fact, he might have been a nephew, or a distant relation. I doubt if many of us would be proud to trot out *everyone* in our family tree. I prefer to hold my thoughts close to my vest until I hear reason to do otherwise."

"That's your prerogative, Albert, and I respect it. I still think the man is no good."

Bob Lesley stares at Bob Jenkins in frank amazement. "If you won't take offense, Bob, I want you to back up those strong opinions. If you ask me you're indicting the fellow without a fair trial."

"Maybe I am. Wife is always accusing me of jumping in too quickly with my opinions. But I think highly of Rose. After the royal treatment she showed us on our trip last spring I hate to see her consorting with anyone with less class than she."

His fellow residents hoot at this and Bob Lesley adds, "Consorting is hardly the term, Bob. They merely drank a cup of coffee in the pub and then walked out together. You don't think he's moving in with her, do you?"

Bob Jenkins answers with vehemence. "I distinctly caught the word 'dinner' and saw that man nodding his head vigorously. I'm convinced Rose has invited him to dinner. Here."

It is Albert Warrington's turn. "You still haven't pinpointed what it is you dislike."

"I'll tell you, Albert. His *manner*. He was shifty, ill at ease, kept hiding his hands. His clothes didn't fit. They were clothes made for someone else. And his shoes. Did either of you notice his shoes?"

His companions shake their heads at Jenkins's question.

"Scuffed, toes cracked. Fellow's done a lot of walking recently. Cheap shoes. Does that speak *quality* to either of you gentlemen?"

Doctor Lesley whistles in amazement. "Bob, I'm speechless, and for a doctor, that in itself is one of the world's small wonders. You are a true observer of humanity, my friend. Worthy of Charles Dickens. I could debate you on the virtues of his clothing, why it might be of poor quality or ill fitting, all that. But your sensing something in his *manner* that you don't like worries me. You certainly make me anticipate dinner tomorrow night. Ellie Johnson is organizing a special table for Rose's return to the dining room. Sort of a 'Welcome

Back to Wynfield' affair. Maybe I'll get lucky and have an opportunity to meet her visitor."

I better alert Ellie, Rose thinks to herself, about the extra guest at tomorrow night's table. Wonder what she'll think about my guest?

Ellie Johnson, as Rose may have predicted, finds the situation hilarious. "Rose McNess, vamp of Wynfield, beauty of the beaches, woman of infinite charms ..."

"Ellie, will you please stop? I am uneasy about having invited this stranger to dinner and you think it is the funniest thing in the world."

"Sorry, Rose, I didn't mean to make a joke out of it. Forgive me. You have to admit; we haven't *had* much excitement around here since you went to the hospital, except for Taki. You, in your inimitable fashion, have just managed to liven things up for us. We need a little spice in our soup."

"Of course I forgive you. But tell me, honestly, am I crazy? Is there something drastically *wrong* with my brain? I am literally amnesiac regarding this man. And any time spent at Virginia Beach."

"You are not crazy, Rose. You're the sanest person in Wynfield Farms. And you are not amnesiac. God, that's an awful label. You're barely out of the hospital and already talking about leading another trip. That's *not* crazy. You've simply blocked that summer out of your mind. Didn't you tell me you got married in 1961? Maybe you had a fling at the beach, felt guilty because you were engaged to be married, and then shook the episode from your memory bank. Emptied the coffers. Could that be the case? You know I'm a marvelous psychiatrist."

"Plausible, Ellie, except for one reason."

"What's that?"

"I was engaged for just two months. I met Tom in October 1961. It was love at first sight and we were married

December 18, 1961. I didn't have a thought in my head about marriage that summer."

"All the more reason to have a fling in July, Rose. Your mysterious stranger is not selling insurance. He is not a friend of either of your late husbands. He says he is *your* old friend. What's done is done, and since you've invited him to dinner tomorrow night, we'll see it through. I say 'we' because I'm going to call those I've asked to sit with us and explain the situation."

"Oh, Ellie, *must* you?"

"I don't *have* to, but I think it's wise. You know from experience that all eyes will be on you and your stranger when you enter the dining room. If there's a core group on Stranger Alert, you'll have a protective circle in place. Besides, we'll all know what questions to ask."

Nodding, Rose agrees. "Logical, Ellie. Who's joining us?"

"I hope this meets with your approval. I've lined up the Puffenbarger twins, Bob Lesley, Lib and Arthur. With your guest, you, and me, that's eight."

"Perfect. The twins will certainly contribute an unusual twist. Who will you bump to accommodate my guest?"

"Frances. She won't mind. She's flexible. I'll explain everything and then let her carry the news to her table. Dinner for tomorrow sounds divine. We're having filet, corn pudding, fresh peas, hot rolls, and parfaits for dessert. God, I'm getting hungry just thinking about it. Why not come on over and let me pull out some cheese and crackers? I'd love to feed you for a change. You've saved my life so many times in the past two years I can't begin to count. Besides we've got to decide what to do about the firecrackers."

"Scrumptious! Cheese and crackers would be wonderful. Eating will be a distraction. I keep thinking there is a key to my past that I should be pursuing."

"Take old Ellie's advice. Don't let this bog you down. After tomorrow night, Conklin will be gone. You've got to look ahead, with hope. And who am I quoting, Rose McNess?"

Rose blushes and blows a silent kiss to her friend.

"Remember telling me that, my first night in from Denver? Something like 'going your own way, having fun, people and projects popping up—and looking ahead with *hope.*' Your very own words, Rose, back to haunt you!"

"Thank you, Ellie, for reminding me of my own philosophy. You are absolutely right, of course, just as *I* was in claiming you as my best friend the moment you arrived. You've made me feel better. You are *truly* a safeguard. My mystery man has popped up and will soon pop out. I'm looking forward to tomorrow evening. Of course I'll come over, Ellie. All this talk about food has made *me* as hungry as a bear. Incidentally, who is *Taki?*"

"*Doctor* Taki Yokamura, our professor. I've just spent the past three hours introducing him to U.S. merchandising techniques."

Rose Mason Meets Rick Conklin
(for the second time in 42 years)

What a nice looking man! Certainly speaks better than he writes. At least he doesn't butcher the King's English. And he does seem sincere. My poor brain: overloaded with the trivia of seventy-plus years. Can't dredge up when or where I ever met Rick. But he says we *did*. I've gone out on a limb with nothing but a person's word before, so this is not much different, I guess. I *am* quite a few years older and should be quite a bit wiser. Am I just so tired that I take the path of least resistance?

CHAPTER
16

Ellie plies Rose with Brie and crackers. She moans several times, "Sure will be glad when you meet a martini you like, Rose."

"That's two of us, Ellie."

"Now about the firecrackers, we must put our minds to it."

"You're right. I know we're correct in not reporting this to Mrs. Gallentine. Taki is due to fly out in two days. We'll snoop and keep it to ourselves until then."

"I have my journal right here. Funny how you remember a favorite professor's words. Fellow back at Old Miss said to 'Write it bold and write it in gold.' Of course, he was talking about class notes. I've carried that in my head all these years. But now, I mean business. I am writing bold."

"Start with Mrs. Gallentine finding the first collection of trash in the hallway, Ellie. That was what, three weeks ago?" Ellie scribbles furiously.

"And the second episode the day after that."

"FIRECRACKERS. May 7. Second floor, right of elevator. Rose, I think our culprit lives on this floor."

"Not necessarily, Ellie. That may be what he wants us to think."

"And it *may* not be a 'he.' I'm sort of thinking one of the twins. You know how they love playing games with each other and sometimes they are rather childish."

"Put them down as a possibility, Ellie. No, I take that back. Don't put any names in writing. We could be hauled into court for libel if this got out."

"What next then, Miss Marple?"

"I'll try walking the halls more, at strange hours. When the suspect is *least* suspecting. And if you continue to keep popping in and out of your place—well, there is no guarantee but we *might* just catch the criminal. Wouldn't that be wonderful! 'Two aging sleuths solve Wynfield Farms mystery.' And if we could do it without informing Mrs. Galantine—all the better! That poor women has enough on her mind trying to get Taki back to Japan. If we're not successful, we'll just set out some bait."

"Bait?" Ellie stops writing and looks at Rose. "Did I hear you correctly?"

"Bait, as in fish. Lure him—or her in. More firecrackers, new matches."

"I'm getting all this down, Rose. Perfect."

"I've had about enough detective work for one afternoon. Tell me about your shopping trip with Taki. I need light entertainment, Ellie."

"Professor Yokamura is such a gentleman. He stood at the top of the escalator and waited for fifteen people to file past him before he got on and floated to the bottom. He enjoyed flying solo on the DOWN escalator."

"He enjoys his privacy. It's a novelty for him. I take it you went to the mall and not Wal-Mart. Did he venture into any stores with you?"

In the next fifteen minutes Ellie elaborated on their store to store adventures in Roanoke's largest shopping mall. After whooping with laughter until she was weak, Rose concludes it's time to leave Ellie and enjoy her privacy. With tears of laughter in her eyes, she slips across to her own apartment.

After a nap, Rose feels hungry again. She decides not to go to the dining room, but to scramble two eggs, warm a croissant in the toaster oven and drink a large glass of milk.

There! I really do feel better. You'd think I'd learn to listen to my empty stomach. Dr. Sellsoe said I should get plenty of calcium if I wanted to keep the rest of my bones in good shape. He'd be proud of me tonight. What a pity I prefer single malt.

A knock at the door halts her clean up of the kitchen.

"Who in the world?" she wonders, glancing at the clock. 7:15. All of her friends are in the dining room, or should be. *No one* misses a meal at Wynfield Farms if they can help it.

"Hold on, I'm coming," she calls. Could Mr. Conklin have gotten the wrong night? She admits to a *frisson* of apprehension as she pulls the door back. Jocey Ribble stands on the threshold.

Rose is flabbergasted. "What a surprise! Come in, come in. I'm delighted to see you Jocey! You must be feeling better. Here, have a seat. I'll take my old favorite."

"Am I interrupting your dinner, Mrs. McNess? I could...could come back at a better time." Jocey looks around the apartment, nervous, ill at ease, her face pinched and drawn.

"No, no dear, I was just finishing. To what do I owe this honor?"

"I hate to bother you, particularly at this hour. But when I didn't see you in the dining room with Mrs. Johnson, I decided to scoot up here. I didn't want to talk to you in front of the others."

The purpose of Jocey's visit still hangs unsaid in the air. "Are you feeling better, Jocey? Forgive my frankness, but you really don't look too well tonight. We've all missed you."

"I hate myself, Mrs. McNess. That's why I've come."

"Jocey, what in the world?"

"I wasn't sick, Mrs. McNess. I lied. I lied to my mother and made her lie to Mrs. Gallentine. I just couldn't face—couldn't face the shame of what I did. Or almost did."

"Jocey, take a deep breath and start from the beginning. That's the only way you are going to make sense. Here, wipe your eyes."

Jocey's eyes are pooling and the tears threaten to puddle and run to her toes. Rose fishes in her cardigan pocket and hands a clean linen handkerchief to the young woman. Jocey dabs at the threatening river.

"Now, Jocey, from the beginning. Either tell me all of your story or *none* of your story. Whichever makes you feel better. I'm a good listener."

Again Jocey sniffs. "The day before yesterday I was working in Montremont, near where you tripped. There was a fellow sitting on the bench, catching his breath. He called to me."

"Was he an older man?"

"No, not old. I would say maybe in his sixties? Younger than you but not by much. Yes, in his sixties. But he was breathing sort of hard like he'd walked a distance and wasn't used to it."

"And? Go on, Jocey, for heaven's sake."

"Well, one thing led to another and he asked if he could take me to lunch and I said, 'Yes.' We ate at the *Skipperjack*, the fish place in Fincastle."

"Hardly a crime, Jocey."

"After lunch he really wanted to, well, have his *way* with me." Her voice confides this in an inaudible whisper.

"Jocey! Did he assault you? Were you in the restaurant? In his car? Where?" Rose's antennae fly up and warning flags wave.

"No, no, not that awful. But he acted like he *would* have if I had given an inch. And I think it was my fault." This brings on a fresh deluge of waterworks.

"Are you saying you *teased* him into this sort of action, Jocey?"

"Oh, no," she cries indignantly. "It was the beer. I made a mistake and had two beers with my lunch. One beer always makes me lightheaded and funny in the belly. *Two* I get positively drunk. I'm so ashamed. That's why I was sick, Mrs. McNess, and let everyone down by not showing up for the

Japanese. I'll never live this down."

"You may not think so tonight, Jocey, or even next week, but you *will* live this down. What you did is *not* your fault. Let's just say you told a white lie for a good reason. And Ellie, Frances and I managed very well in your greenhouse. I just hope we put things back properly. If anyone is at fault here, it is the man who was loitering in our garden. Are you sure he didn't do anything *else* to you Jocey, other than wound your pride?"

"Oh I'm sure, Mrs. McNess. And at first, I was taken in by him. He's charming and good looking. Nice smile and all. And when he said he knew you, I thought, 'Well, he has to be a nice guy if he knows Mrs. McNess.' He said he was coming here to pay you a surprise visit. Asked all about you but told me not to mention that I'd seen him. And here I am blabbing on about him. What does *that* make me, Mrs. McNess?"

"Jocey, he's paid me his *surprise* visit. He came by this morning. Rick Conklin is a man I knew from Virginia Beach years ago." Rose hopes she is saying this in a calm voice.

"That's him! And he's back to lifeguard in Virginia, after all this time. I told him I thought he was a little old but he—"

"Jocey, did he tell you anything else about himself? Or where he was from? I'm having the devil's own time placing Mr. Conklin. I simply cannot recall one minute of our friendship. I *hope* that is all it was."

"He said he was from Detroit, and went on and on about being a lifeguard. Would you mind if I told you one more thing Mrs. McNess?"

"After what we've shared this evening, Jocey, would 'one more thing' really matter?"

"You may not want to hear this, Mrs. McNess, especially if he's a good friend. But I don't trust Mr. Conklin. He has steely blue eyes. And he was too nice, in a smarmy sort of way."

"Smarmy? Pardon me, Jocey, but I'm not familiar with that particular adjective."

"You may not know the word, Mrs. McNess, but you

know the type: a man who wants too much from you too fast. Moves in with all sorts of sweet sayings and flatters a girl off her feet and into bed before you can say 'Bingo!'"

"I've got the picture, Jocey."

"He wasn't your type, Mrs. McNess. He didn't look like the kind of folks you take to. His clothes didn't fit. Almost as if he'd picked them up from a thrift shop. *He* looked second-hand."

"I'll have to defend him there, Jocey. He looked very presentable this morning. Clean shirt, clean trousers. Every inch a gentleman. Perhaps you saw him in his work clothes."

"That's another thing I didn't like. His fingernails were filthy."

"An honest day's work, Jocey?" Rose unwittingly plays the Devil's advocate to Jocey's every description.

"I hate to be so down on this fellow, but when he said he was going to look you up I thought I just had to come and warn you. But since you've already met him, I guess by now he is on his way to Colonial Beach. He was having his car repaired. Said all he wanted to do was renew his friendship with you. It was stupid of me to come up here."

"No, Jocey. I've not seen the last of him. I invited him to dinner tomorrow evening. Here, in the Wynfield Dining Room."

"Here? Mrs. McNess, can't you get out of it?" Jocey shrieks in alarm.

"I assure you Jocey, he's not going to try anything fishy with *this* old lady. I have no intention of calling it off. He's invited to dinner and he shall come to dinner. He was a part of my past once and I hope to learn more about that over soup and salad. An extra course for the mystery dinner."

"I'm glad I won't be there, Mrs. McNess. He's full of blarney, if you'll forgive me saying so."

"I've heard worse, Jocey. It's time for me to face the music. What you have just told me tonight is *our* secret. Let's not mention this to Mrs. Gallentine. Professor Yokamura is causing enough ripples. Mrs. Gallentine is very protective of each of us. She'd call out the National Guard if she thinks my friend is a trouble-maker."

"Mrs. Gallentine sees the residents as I see my seed-
lings: each one has to be nurtured and cultivated and settled
in the proper surroundings. Beware of predators. Remember, you're not back to being settled, Mrs. McNess. *You* should
beware."

"Jocey, you're a sensitive person. I hate it that someone took advantage of you, especially an acquaintance of
mine. Now, it's my bedtime. Thank you for coming tonight,
my dear. Let's both keep our secret. Things will look better in
the morning, I promise."

"You'll be careful, won't you?" asked Jocey, hugging
her friend.

"I certainly will, Jocey. Thank you again." Rose returns
the hug and watches Jocey run the length of the corridor
and down the steps. Something is not right. Rose wants to
believe her, yet she has the feeling she has not heard the
complete story. Her intuition tells her that Mr. Conklin has
been more forward than Jocey admits. After all, she is pretty,
actually a *very* pretty young woman.

Pshaw! He can hardly present a menace to me. I hope
I'm able to sleep tonight and not spend hours racking my
brain uncovering scraps of information about Mr. Conklin.
'Renew an old friendship.' Maybe I should have Annie's Jim
check his background. I'm too tired to think about that *and*
solve the firecracker mystery. What is the prayer my children used to say when they were little?

> *Four corners to my bed,*
> *Four angels round my head:*
> *One to watch,*
> *One to pray,*
> *And two to bear my soul away.*

If it's all the same to you, Lord, I think I'll just settle for
the two angels to watch and pray. I can't spare my soul right
now.

Rose Cogitates after her Session with Jocey

How my heart aches for that poor child! A desperately ill father, a mother who depends on her for everything, and now my 'friend' who takes advantage of her! And yet, as sorry as I am that Jocey's lunch date turned out so badly, I am convinced that she enjoyed Rick's attentions. And she swears that he didn't harm her in any way. How could he? Broad daylight in the town of Fincastle? Public restaurant where people were coming and going all the time? I should have given Jocey that little poem I keep framed by my bedside...

Ain't the Roses Sweet
This world that we're a-livin' in,
Is mighty hard to beat:
You git a thorn with every rose,
*But ain't the roses sweet!**

*From the writings of Frank L. Stanton

CHAPTER

17

Rose finds a comfortable position and begs for sleep's sweet oblivion. She turns left, then right. Tonight the familiar mattress feels like a pallet of corn shucks, foreign to ever muscle and joint in her fragile body. Water! I need water. She struggles for balance, straightens and sits for a minute on the edge of the bed. Gripping the faithful walker Rose starts for the kitchen.

This is when a dram of single malt would be nectar. I'll just settle for Wynfield water. Why am I so thirsty tonight?

Rose carefully takes the water into the living room. She sinks into her favorite chair, the memory of Jocey's tear streaked face fresh in her mind. I was married to a lawyer for too many years, Rose reflects. There is more here than has been told. Rick may have spurned Jocey and she became irritated, or perhaps he wasn't attentive enough, On the other hand, perhaps his advances were overwhelming and she simply didn't know how to handle him. For heaven's sakes, Jocey is thirty-something if she's a day. She's bound to know what men want and she trusted him enough to accept a luncheon invitation. Probably glad for the attention. Not that I'm an expert on Jocey's love life. Or anyone's love life for that matter. Well, what's done is done and Mr. Conklin will be here soon enough. I better shuffle back to bed if I want to sleep at all tonight. Thinking a moment of the restless hour she'd just endured, Rose says decisively, "I'll bring my quilt and sleep here! This squashy old seat fits my bum to a 'T'."

Just as she crawls into the arms of Morpheous, she hears a bell clanging, hiccupping loud repetitive staccato bursts with increasing and insistent intensity.

"Oh, good Lord," Rose cries, "the fire alarm!"

Ellie pounds into her apartment, "Rose! Let me help you! Where is your robe? We've got to get out. Oh, God, you can't manage the steps and the elevator's out. Come on Rose, let's move. Who knows where this fire started?"

"Is it on Two, Ellie?"

"No time to think, Rose. Grab your purse. Pray we'll find a couple of men at the end of the corridor. They'll make a seat for you. And poor Vinnie! I bet Major Featherstone is scared to death."

"No, he's not," jokes Rose. "My guess is he's directing traffic. I'm ready. Close that door tightly if you will. I don't want to lose everything."

The corridor is dense with thick white smoke. Rose and Ellie cling to each other. They join an orderly procession of residents, each carrying a treasured possession or pet, or in some cases, both. They file rapidly, silently down the stairway. Jim Greider and Charlie Caldwell join hands in a chair grip and tenderly transport Rose sedan chair style to the Reception Room. The others she joins are equally as bewildered and sleepy.

Rose perches uncomfortably on a stiff-backed chair as Vinnie Featherstone wheels toward her.

"Rose, Rose, wouldn't this happen now, with two of us needing help with the steps? Bless Father Charlie, that's all I can say."

"And Jim Greider," adds Rose. "I hope Bob Jenkins gets someone to help him with Esther. Oh, there go more firemen, up the back entrance to Two. Any idea where the fire started, Vinnie?"

"No, but the major will know. He's upstairs directing traffic."

"Of course." Rose laughs aloud at the thought of the scenario. "I knew we could count on the major to direct this campaign."

Vinnie resembles a large pink marshmallow this evening. From the satin bow around her soft, white waves to the graceful peignoir and the tips of her pom-pommed slippers, she is a pink sunrise. "Has anyone seen Mrs. Gallentine?" she asks.

"I'm sure she's here," Rose reassures her.

Residents mill around in various nightdress, hugging their possessions and making small talk as if this were cocktail hour. It's hardly a scene charged with anxiety or fear. Conversations rise and fall in a steady drone, punctuated often with outbursts of loud and nervous laughter and shouts of "Can you believe this?" The acrid odor of smoke, so pervasive and heavy in the upper corridor a half hour previously, has all but disappeared.

As a magician might conjure a rabbit from a sleeve, suddenly Mrs. G. materializes in the center of the room. Rose notes that her night attire is as fashionably elegant as her daytime apparel.

"Ladies and gentlemen, dear friends, dear Wynfielders." The resident director is shouting. She has pulled over a square hassock and climbed upon it, elevating her even further.

"The fire is *out*. Firemen are using giant fans to blow the smoke through windows on Two West. All danger is over. Twenty more minutes and you are free to return to your apartments."

"Where did the fire start, Mrs. Gallentine?"

"Yes, what *is* the origin?"

"Electrical failure?"

"We're not sure of the cause or exactly *where* it started, but rest assured, it will be investigated." Mrs. Gallentine is the picture of calm as she speaks to the group.

Ellie sidles up to Rose and whispers, "What did I tell you? *Our firecracker fiend* is at work."

"You may be correct, Ellie. This incident might smoke him out. Literally. Where is Taki? Have you seen him tonight?"

"Father Charlie has him in tow. Taki probably loves all this excitement."

Then, in a moment both wildly unexpected and predictably inevitable, Henrietta Puffenbarger, stuffed into her blue and green plaid flannel wrapper and resembling a much loved, much worn Christmas teddy bear, pads up to Mrs. Gallentine and tugs her arm for attention.

"I confess. I'm the guilty party. I am responsible for the fire and all of this terrible confusion. I put a pan of cocoa on the burner and then, well, I must have forgotten it. I—I may have dozed off. All of this is my fault and I am so sorry."

The group is in a forgiving mood. Many of the residents surged forward to speak to Henrietta. The twin's eyes fill with tears but her dignity remains intact. This teddy bear is well loved.

Mrs. Gallentine has a lightning flash, an inspiration of genius, one of those rarely-to-be-seized upon opportunities when one asks, *why not?* "I shall open *The Rose and The Grape.* After tonight's scare, I think we could all enjoy a small dram of sherry. Strictly for medicinal purposes, of course. The party is on me!" Paula Gallentine looks around the room. "Harriet? Henrietta? Rose? Anyone game or are you eager to return to bed?"

"Well, well," chuckles Charlie Caldwell. "Who'd a thought this would ever happen at Wynfield Farms? Three in the morning and we're pub crawling! Coming, Rose? I'm your transportation home so you can't leave the party before I say the word."

"Charlie Caldwell, you know perfectly well I'm able to take the elevator after this. But what a happy ending to what might have been a disaster. Of course I'll join you!

"Mrs. Gallentine, anything alcoholic is officially off-limits to me, but I cannot think that a drop or two of Bristol cream could harm this new hip. Just a wee drop, for celebratory purposes. You've turned a bad scene into good. Bless you!"

·TREASURES:
Wynfield Residents and
What They Saved The Night Of The Fire

Rose McNess: Black leather purse with sixteen dollars and eight cents; checkbook; door key, latest album of family photos.

Ellie Johnson: Favorite red wig in black and white checked hatbox.

Charlie Caldwell: *Bible* (King James Version) and *Book of Common Prayer* presented to him in Salisbury, North Carolina when he was confirmed at age 12. Carved war club retrieved from Solomon Islands during Navy duty in WWII.

Albert Warrington: Eye drops, two never-worn cravats from Brooks Brothers; black satchel containing taxidermy and sculpting tools.

Bob Jenkins: Esther (and her night nurse); pedometer.

Lib Everett: L.L. Bean bag with five unfinished Christmas stockings and assorted needlepoint paraphernalia; biography of Edith Wharton.

Arthur Everett: Marriage certificate (framed) from Oxford, England; favorite edition (original Greek) of Homer's *Iliad.*

Harriet Puffenbarger: New golf putter and worn copy of *Fanny Farmer's Cookbook* (first edition).

Henrietta Puffenbarger: One (1) potholder (scorched).

Jana Zdorek: Lucy the poodle.

Vinnie Featherstone: New jar of *Helia D* face cream (imported).

Major Featherstone: Vinnie.

Frances Keynes-Livingston: Hohner accordion and packet of airmail letters from England.

18

Rick Conklin knocks on Rose's door at six precisely. He had been lucky in hitching a ride. The drug rep heading to Clifton Forge dropped Rick at the Wynfield gates less than ten minutes ago. He glances at his shoes. The loafers are not new but hold a shine better than the old brown oxfords and the soles are decent, as if anyone might care.

Rick looks presentable and he knows it. Small beads of sweat moisten his upper lip and he is wiping them away when the door opens.

"Good evening, Mr. Conk—I mean, *Rick*. Please, come in."

Rose appraises her guest and her eyebrows lift in approval. His navy blazer is pressed, gray trousers are creased and the regimental stripe tie he wears is so correct it could have been plucked from the Albert Warrington Tree of Ties. Broad and confident shoulders easily fill out the coat and his posture is erect.

Clothes may not make the man, but they certainly help. Rick Conklin is very handsome. Why did I work myself into such a stew? "You're right on time," she says aloud.

"*You* did say six, didn't you Rose? I try to be punctual. If I'm too early, just say the word—"

"No, no, six it is. We usually have a toddy upstairs before dinner. I can't drink of course, as I explained the other morning, but you're welcome to imbibe."

"Don't mind if I do. Show me where you keep your whiskey and I'll pour myself a neat one. Nice place you got here, Rose." He looks around admiringly.

"My liquor cabinet is here, under the odds and ends drawer. Just pull it out. Everything's there, so help yourself, please. I did mention we usually have wine with dinner, didn't I?"

"You did. Don't worry, I won't drink too much. I'm a man known to hold his liquor."

"By whom?" Rose asks.

"What d'ya mean?"

"By *whom* are you known to hold your liquor? Just a rhetorical question." She changes the subject before he can comment. "You know, Rick, except for your telling me we met at Virginia Beach, I have no idea where you hail from or where you are living now. I'm sure my friends will inquire this evening."

"We aren't having dinner alone?"

Is it Rose's imagination or did a stricken look cross the man's face? Rose laughs and says, "Heavens no. The Wynfield Dining room doesn't even have tables for two. No *tête a tête* dining here. Six good friends are joining us. In fact, this evening is my 'welcome back' to the regular world. Real world is perhaps a better way to put it, after my fall. You'll enjoy all of my friends. But I warn you, several are even older than I, if possible."

Rick chooses to ignore this last comment for his next question is, "Do I look all right? I sure don't want to embarrass you, Rose."

"Impeccable, Rick. Now, bring your drink and sit. Tell me about yourself." Rose notices that her guest's drink is a full one. No ice tinkles in his glass of bourbon.

"Let's see. I've lived in Detroit for the past twelve years. Before that, I was in Minnesota. I've moved around a lot, like you."

"Did you ever marry, Rick?"

"Once. Nice gal. Just didn't work out."

"No children, I gather?"

"Nah. Lucky on that score. These your kids in the pictures?"

He had been scanning the family groups on her table.

"Yes, my three children and the six grands. I've been very fortunate in my life."

"I knew you would be. You were that kind of girl forty years ago. You had your head on straight. Always teased me about—"

A sharp knock stops their conversation.

"That will be my across-the-hall neighbor, Ellie Johnson," she whispers then, "Come in, Ellie."

Rick scrambles to his feet and offers his hand to Ellie.

"Ellie Johnson, Mr. Conklin. *Rick* Conklin, that is. Ellie is the nice person organizing tonight's dinner party."

"Oh, sure. Should we be getting down there now?"

"No, no," Rose assures him. "You were telling me that I *teased* you about something at the beach—"

"Forget it. Slip of the tongue."

"Tell me, Rick. Any little detail that might trigger this old memory of mine is welcome. Come on, what did I tease you about?"

"Don't be bashful in front of me, Rick," gushes Ellie. She has been sizing up Rose's visitor. "Rose and I have absolutely no secrets. Not even about our past."

"The sad thing is, Ellie, I cannot remember a past that included Rick. I was trying to squeeze more details out of him when I got sidetracked. You were telling me you lived in Detroit. Were you with Ford?"

"In a manner of speaking, yes."

"Ah! A captain of industry, I knew it!" grins Ellie.

"Hardly that," Rick Conklin confesses, looking appropriately shy. "I can't talk about my job too much. You see, I'm taking a leave of absence for the summer and it would never do if anyone up there got wind of it. The less said about Detroit, the better."

Rick Conklin, Chief Engineer on the Greenfield Village Railway in Dearborn, Michigan, had been fired for insubor-

dination two weeks prior to his arrival in Virginia. His co-
workers at Greenfield had rejoiced to see the back of him
and couldn't care less if he talked about his *former* job. Rick
hopes he sounds convincing to Rose and her nosy friend.

"So you're a Midwesterner, Rick?" Ellie inquires.

"You might say. I was born in South Dakota but I've
drifted east."

"How in the world did you end up in Virginia? And as a
lifeguard? Not once, but twice. I find that the rarest of coincidences, don't you, Rose?"

Bless Ellie's heart. She is asking all the politically correct questions. I just don't seem capable of focusing on anything tonight. Ellie will get more information out of Rick than
I ever could. Oh, thank you, dear friend, for coming to my
rescue. What did I tease him about? He avoided me on that
twice. Rather secretive, in fact.

"I don't want to rush you two, but I think we should
mosey down. It takes me longer, you realize. Rick, do you
need the lavatory before we go?"

"Nope."

"Fine. Ellie, after you."

They make their way slowly down the corridor: Ellie,
Rose slowly pushing her walker, Rick bringing up the rear.

"Instead of *Dinner at Eight,* we are 'dinner for eight'," Ellie
offers brightly. "Who wrote that play, Rose, do you recall?"

"Not I. Maybe Rick does. Do you remember, Rick, who
wrote *Dinner at Eight?*"

"I don't go in much for plays and stuff. No time for it,"
he stammers.

Ellie breezes over this gaffe. "I know that Alexander
Wolcott starred in it. Or was that *The Man Who Came to Dinner?* Who's fuzzyheaded now, Rose? You two take the elevator. I'll run on down and steer our crowd to the table. It's the
one in the corner, Rose, north wall."

Ellie trots down the stairs, eager to catch Bob Lesley
and the Everetts. He's no intellectual heavy weight, that's for
sure. Certainly don't want to embarrass the poor man by

talking about the theatre and I doubt he's big on literature either. Hard on Lib, the librarian. Wonder what cheerful conversational gambits she'll dream up? And the Puffenbargers. They would challenge a billy goat!

Ellie has no more time to contemplate. When she reaches their table, she discovers Jocey arranging a centerpiece.

"Superb, Jocey. Did you know Rose has a special guest this evening? A mystery man."

Jocey looks at Ellie as if she were an alien. "Jocey, what is it?" Ellie asks, dumbfounded.

"She didn't cancel her invitation to that man?"

"Cancel? Heavens, no. There he is now, at the door with Rose." Ellie gestures toward the wide doors, where Rose and Rick are now entering.

"Hope your dinner goes just fine." The horticulturist slips like mercury between the gathering clusters of residents and disappears through the kitchen entrance.

Dinner does go 'just fine'. Rose introduces her guest as an 'old friend from the past' and that seems to satisfy everyone. Rick chats easily and asks questions of the residents. Particularly intrigued by the Puffenbarger twins, he asks about their hobbies. Upon learning that they are natives of Botetourt County, he asks how long their family has lived in the area and whether or not they were all farmers. He is less effusive with Lib and Arthur, but then, as Rose reasons, Arthur's Latin quotations and polished dome of a head are off-putting to some, and Lib is being unusually quiet and pensive.

Bob Lesley delights in his role as quasi-master of ceremonies. He flirts shamelessly with Ellie *and* Rose and makes no secret of his admiration for the latter. He is generous with the carafe of wine, lamenting the fact that Rose is not yet able to join the toasts he proposes. But mainly he excels in his discussions with Rose's guest.

"Rick, do I understand from Rose that you are applying for a lifeguard job here in Virginia? Tell me about that."

"That's right, Dr. Lesley. I spent a lot of time in the Detroit library and they carry newspapers from all over the country. Found this article in *The Roanoke Times*. Always liked reading the Virginia papers. I had a good time here in the '60s."

"That so? I understand you and Rose met back then. Quite a few years ago. Interesting, I saw the self-same article you mention. Kids today don't want to work, isn't that it? But good Lord, man, not to sound demeaning, but you're almost as old as I am."

Rick grins broadly, showing even teeth slightly yellowed but still intact. "I'm close to sixty-one. And I bench press 200 pounds. I try to keep myself fit."

"Good heavens," sighs Arthur Everett. "I doubt if anyone around here has ever *seen* someone who can bench press 200 pounds. What is your line of work, Mr. Conklin? Or are you, as with others at this table, retired from gainful employment?"

"I still keep my hand in. Back in Detroit. Sort of halfway retired you might say."

"And exactly what *is* your line of work?" persists Arthur.

"Engineering."

Rose is feeling radiant about dinner. Jocey's flowers—does Rick know Jocey has arranged them?—add a festive touch, her friends have rallied to her support in this potentially awkward situation, and she is very much at peace in the familiar setting.

There remains a small amount of red wine and dessert to be enjoyed.

"Who bids for this last drop of wine?" Bob Lesley gently lifts the near-empty carafe and searches the seven smiling faces around him.

Rick Conklin reaches past Rose to take the carafe and in doing so his left arm shoots out of his sleeve and exposes his bare wrist.

The blood drains from Rose's face. She is rigid and shaking as if a glacial shock had overwhelmed her.

Ellie cries out, "Rose, sweetie! You're as white as the tablecloth. What's wrong? Bob, Rose needs help!"

Bob Lesley leaps from his seat and crouches by Rose. With a physician's deft touch he places his hand on Rose's wrist and checks her pulse.

Rick Conklin, clearly bewildered at the meteoric turn of events, is rooted to his chair. What is happening? His legs become as immobile as tree trunks. What is happening?

Bob Lesley seizes command of the situation. He barks, "We've got to get Rose to her room. Rose, can you hear me? Shall I call Clinic for a stretcher?"

Fortunately, the dining room has now emptied, and only this one table remains to wonder what has struck their friend. Rose slowly begins to emerge from her trance. She is aware of the present and more than aware of what had occurred in the past—some forty years ago.

"No stretcher, Bob, please. So sorry...end the evening... Just help me to my apartment and let me get...warm. I ... I can manage." Her voice is trembling and so weak that Bob Lesley leans close to listen.

"Rick and I can support you, Rose. Ellie, get the walker. We'll have you home in no time."

"Not Rick. Arthur. Please." Rose speaks softly but Bob Lesley hears determination in her voice.

"Rick, Rose doesn't want to offend you. Would you mind seeing the Puffenbargers to their home, then joining us at Rose's? I'm sure she will want to tell you good night. Arthur, lend me a hand here?"

"*Experto credite,*" the scholar replies, joining Bob Lesley at Rose's side.

"No Latin, Arthur," his wife chides. "I'll not go up. Rose has enough people to fuss over her. I'll check in tomorrow, Rose." She swiftly makes her way out of the dining room.

"We'll get you home in no time, Rose," Bob Lesley reassures her. "You're doing fine. Bet you'll be using a cane next week."

"*Consule Planco.* Ah, for those times."

"What are you muttering, Arthur?" asks Rose, her voice gaining timbre as they reach the elevator.

"I merely stated that I longed, we all longed, for the good old days. Our carefree youth."

Rose shivers. "My *youth* is my problem tonight."

"You must be feeling better, Rose," confirms the doctor as he opens the door to Rose's apartment. He helps her into the wing chair and states, "Your sense of humor is returning. Where might I find a blanket? You're still shivering and your pulse is too rapid. Any aspirin around?"

"I know where both items are, Doc," calls Ellie, disappearing into the bedroom. She returns in a moment with a quilt and places it around her friend, tucking in the corners tenderly as one would cover a napping child. She produces water and two aspirin, offering them to the physician.

"Take these, Rose. I hesitate to give you any unauthorized tranquilizers, but aspirin should help. Wish I could prescribe a good shot of brandy. Shall I call your surgeon?"

"No, no, that's not necessary." Rose manages a small laugh. "I'll recover, Bob, and I do thank you and Arthur. Now, both of you get on your way. Ellie will stay with me. I want her here when Mr. Conklin returns."

"Are you sure you don't want a man around, Rose?" Arthur is convinced that Rose's visitor was the sole cause of her panic attack. "I'll be happy to stay. Can't bench press 200 but I *am* a man."

This evokes a grin. "No, no, Arthur, both of you go on. This is something Ellie and I can handle."

Reluctantly the two men exit, shaking their heads and talking conspiratorially as they pad down the corridor toward home.

Ellie sits across from Rose and grasps both her hands in her own, and pleads, "Honey, what in the world came over you?" she pleads.

"I remembered *everything*, Ellie. Something clicked in my brain when I saw it."

"Saw *what?*" begs Ellie.

"Rick Conklin's tattoo. There, on his left wrist. A blue cobra twisting around his left wrist. When he reached for the carafe, his cuffs shot back and there it was. I couldn't believe it. You know how your brain 'freezes' when you drink something icy cold? My brain has been frozen for forty years. The incident caused a block, call it *amnesia*, if you wish, in my mind. When I saw that horrible twisting blue snake, my ice block melted. Everything came flooding back. I didn't want the men to be here when Rick Conklin returns. What he did was shameful, but I don't want to humiliate him completely when I confront him with the truth."

"What *did* the man do, Rose? Rape you? Is that what you remembered?"

"No, no, Ellie. Wait until he returns. I don't have the strength to tell this twice."

In a matter of minutes, Rick Conklin knocks softly at the door and lets himself in.

"How're you feeling, Rose? God, you gave us all a scare. Those old sisters won't get over this meal soon. Some ending."

"Sit down, Reed Chenowski."

Rick's face mirrors his fears. For a second he is speechless "I, I, don't know who—"

"Don't add *lying* to your list of cowardly acts. It all came back to me, Reed, in one instant at the table. Do you remember taking the carafe of wine from Dr. Lesley?"

"Yeah. Just helping the Doc play host."

Rose continues. "That one move unlocked a torrent of memories. Your wrist shot out and I saw the blue snake. I remembered my weekend in Virginia Beach, I remembered going with you to Dot's for crab cakes, I remembered the bathing suit I wore, but mostly I remembered my friend, Alice Smith. And I remembered the afternoon of the storm. She drowned. Along with Rick Conklin."

"No! It was Reed who died."

Suddenly he jumps to his feet and shouts, "I'm Rick."

"Show me your left wrist, Reed."

Rose's eyes command the man to sit, to roll up his left

shirtsleeve.

Reed obeys, and there, above the wide watch band on his left wrist is the screaming blue tattoo of a writhing snake.

"Earlier tonight you said I teased you about something. That started my mind turning ever so slowly. Years ago I told you that someday you were going to regret having gotten that tattoo. That people in business didn't do that sort of thing. Rick didn't have a tattoo. And Alice was crazy about him. She was hoping he'd ask her for a date that last afternoon. Instead, he died trying to save her. Some irony. And you, you were the stronger swimmer. I had seen you in the ocean, you and Rick, and you outdistanced him by ten lengths. Why didn't you go after Alice?"

Reed puts his hands to his head and they can hear him begin to sob quietly.

Ignoring the pitiful specimen cowed on her sofa, Rose continues, "I remember begging you to go after Rick and Alice. I knew that if you reached Rick the two of you might have a chance to rescue Alice. And then, nothing. The rest is blank. Later I was told that I passed out."

Not meeting her eyes, Reed states "You collapsed on the sand."

"Were you the one who carried me to the lifeguards' shed?"

"Yes," Reed answers in a restrained voice. "When I got you back to the shed, people were running for shelter. You were soaked from the rain. I placed you on the cot and someone covered you with a blanket. You had passed out."

"Then what did you do, Reed?"

"I knelt beside you for two, three minutes. You were breathing hard but steady. I must've panicked because I remembered Rick and that girl. I ran back to the water's edge and I could see the Beach Patrol's boat racing toward a spot in the distance. You could barely hear its motor above the storm. Eventually the boat returned with one body: your girl friend. Rick's body was gone forever in that ocean."

"Alice. Her name was Alice Smith. She was to begin

teaching in Roanoke with me that September. What happened next, Reed?"

"I ran back to the shed. I can still smell the stink of too many hot, wet bodies crowded into that cesspool of a shelter. They must've thought you were a goner, too, until you started coughing and screaming.

"I grabbed for my clothes on the peg. People were shouting and shaking you and screaming for the Beach Patrol and all hell was breaking loose. Like I say, I grabbed for my clothes, only they were *Rick's* clothes: his faded polo shirt, khaki jacket, his jeans, with a wallet stuffed deep inside the pocket. I didn't choose Rick's clothes on purpose. I just grabbed what I could. All I remember is taking the wad of bills from Rick's wallet and leaving it in the pocket of *my* jeans hanging on the peg. Guess someone found that later. Must've been over five hundred bucks. Then I checked to see if you were okay. You were sitting up and coughing by this time, so I took off."

"In that split second, Reed, you stole Rick's identity?"

"Yeah."

"You stole not only his possessions but his *name?*" asks Ellie, stunned and speaking for the first time.

"But not his money, lady. I panicked. I left the money and I split."

"Do you have any idea why you became Rick Conklin?" Rose prods.

"I tell you... I honestly don't know whether I meant to do it or if it was an accident. My heart was beatin' so hard I can still feel how it beat that day. Maybe I did it for a reason. I don't know. Rick always seemed to have everything I didn't. Not just lots of money, but he knew the score. Knew that he'd *be* somebody in life. Maybe I thought I could become the man he was going to be."

"But why did you come back, Reed? Why did you look me up after forty years?"

"Until yesterday, the last memory I had of you, Rose, was cradling you in my arms and placing you on that damp cot. I stroked your cheek with my fingers and said goodbye.

Then a lot of people started crowding around. But I never stopped thinking about you, Rose. I loved you. You thought I was a poor dumb hick. Maybe I was, but I really had feelings for you. That's why I had to look you up, to see if those feelings were still here." Reed points to his chest.

"And that's it?" asks Rose, not moving.

"And to ask your forgiveness. I've felt so guilty all these years. And I kept asking myself what if I'd jumped in the water after Rick? What if I'd drowned? Would Rose have married Rick? What if I'd been able to save one of them? Or both? And I did nothing. Guilt and shame, Rose. That's what I'll carry to my grave."

"I couldn't, as a Christian, sit here and say I cannot forgive you, Reed. I'm trying to fit all the pieces of this puzzle together. You came here tonight without deception, except for the name. Did you ever think what news of Rick's death would do to his family?"

"Rick was an orphan. No one would miss him. And my family had never tried to locate me; I'd been gone to them for over six years. Rick and Reed, lost forever to folks who didn't give a good damn. Sorry. And it's God's own truth, I still don't know whether I did it deliberately... or if it just happened."

"I believe you, Reed. I recall now that it was a terrible storm, a nor'easter. No one could have survived very long in those waves. Alice wanted Rick and she got him. In death."

Ellie shudders. "This is too much for two old women. You've accomplished your purpose here, Reed. Now, I think it's time for you to leave. Don't you agree, Rose?"

"I certainly do, Ellie. Reed, good night, and goodbye. Perhaps you'll save two lives at Colonial Beach this summer. That would be sweet redemption. Your forgiveness would be complete." .

For the first time in the past twenty minutes, Reed Chenowski smiles. "Thank you, Rose Mason." He touches her upturned cheek with his fingers and walks out into the night.

A Few of the Unspoken and Unwritten Reactions to Rose McNess's Dinner Guest

Harriet Puffenbarger: I wonder how far this nice man hits a golf ball?

Henrietta Puffenbarger: What a strong young man! I bet he was a real Lothario on the beach!

Lib Everett: The fellow must be pretty smart to get by on his wits as he has for sixty-one years. Why couldn't I come up with a good nautical adventure to recommend for his beach reading?

Arthur Everett: Pleasant chap, dressed well enough. Definitely not our Rose's type.

Bob Lesley: A bit shifty: no direct eye contact with any of us. Yet he's well spoken. Bench-presses 200 pounds?

Ellie Johnson: I've seen Rick Conklin's type before; they're all cut from the same cloth: trouble. Sure hope Rose sees the light and cans this guy.

CHAPTER

19

Rose and Ellie sit in silence, each so conflicted by private and tumultuous thoughts they fear revealing them aloud. Ellie is the first to give voice to her agitation.

"Mr. Chenowski's confession would've been touching if this whole episode weren't so tragic. Rose, I'm spending the night here. Right on the sofa. No argument, no discussion. Let me zip over and change into my nightclothes. You are not to be alone tonight."

"You know something, Ellie? I won't refuse. I'd like having someone here with me. As much as I hate to give into weakness, encountering my past has been a shock. I'm as limp as a piece of wet blotting paper."

"It's been a shock to *me* too, Rose, and I don't even have a new hip. You were far more magnanimous with that man than I would have been. Imagine, taking a dead man's clothes *and* his name and living that life forever. Remind me not to go swimming at Colonial Beach this summer, particularly if Mr. Conklin gets that job."

"Chenowski. Reed Chenowski. And I hope I soon forget him completely. But isn't it ironic that he is applying for a job as lifeguard again? Almost seems like he *wants* to absolve himself of that horrible cloud of cowardice."

"And guilt. Don't forget *guilt*, Rose. Sit here while I run across the hall. When I return I'll help you get into bed. I'll even toss in a back rub."

Rose clutches the quilt close and looks out at the starless night. How bizarre that this tragedy could lodge in her brain for over forty years and then roar out with furious velocity at seeing the tattoo. The tattoo—an ugly key to the rusty lock on a door that had long refused to open. Rose shakes her head, as if to dislodge any further memories lurking up there.

Every minute of that weekend in Virginia Beach now seems vivid and real. How could that be? What has lain dormant for so long needs to be explained, to be disposed of, yes, confronted.

Rose fondles her soapstone rabbit and waits for Ellie to return. She closes her eyes and slips back to Virginia Beach, July, 1961.

She and Alice drove from Roanoke in Rose's small red sedan, happy to escape city heat for a carefree, cool weekend in the popular resort. Alice had made the reservations; three nights to avoid the Sunday afternoon traffic. Everyone assured her that leaving the beach on Monday morning was a piece of cake compared to the nightmare of Sunday afternoon departures.

Rose recalls the modest, brown two-story boarding house that Alice had chosen. Was it a Mrs. Dorman who owned it? It was one street away from the board walk; "Guaranteed Quiet" was their tag. It was brown on the outside and the inside, with long, beige curtains at the windows. Lining the parlor walls were brown bookcases filled with volumes whose worn bindings hinted more of second hand bookshops than avid readers. There were complete sets of Dickens, Thackeray, Hardy and Sherlock Holmes. She and Alice had giggled and agreed that no one in their right mind would pick such literary heavy weights for beach-side reading.

But the room upstairs, also beige, was clean and cheap. Rose remembers a square, faded picture of two kittens playing with a ball of yarn. Was that in our room or in the hallway leading to the shared bathroom?

That first afternoon she and Alice had changed and headed for the ocean. It was nearly two when they unrolled towels and got settled on the sand. Neither girl had noticed the lifeguard stand directly to one side. They had been so busy talking and gawking that they didn't realize where they had positioned themselves.

Rose suggested moving, but Alice had whispered that this was a good omen and "maybe they'd get lucky and meet a fella."

Alice Smith was from the tiny hamlet of Iris, Virginia. For Alice, the city of Roanoke was the equivalent of New York, London and Los Angeles piled into one gigantic ice cream sundae. The Atlantic Ocean was the cherry on top. Whatever the beach offered a girl, Alice was here to take advantage of it.

"Aren't you supposed to have a beautiful life with romance and adventure? Maybe find men at the beach? Aren't girls supposed to get dressed up in the evening and let guys take them out? First dinner, then the amusement park, and a little smooching after that?" Never more than smooching. Alice was a babe in the woods when it came to men, but she was a good girl and she had made it plain to Rose that she knew when to say no. Life was not supposed to include remorse or shame for unseemly behavior. She owed her parents that much.

She and Alice had gone into the water eventually, she to swim and Alice to sit in the shallow pools at the edge of the sand. When she returned, Alice was talking to one of the lifeguards—Rick.

Rick explained his duties as Alice sat and listened intently, head cocked to one side and smiling coyly at the proper times. His buddy, Reed, who beckoned to Rose, joined them. The four walked back to the lifeguards' stand.

Rose told them she would see them later and strolled over to her towel to sun herself.

She looked up a few minutes later to see Reed standing next to her. The first thing she noticed was his tattoo, a horrid blue snake twisting around his left wrist. It disgusted her. She knew she shouldn't show disdain quite as strongly as she felt, so she teased him about it. Rose couldn't remember the exact words when she asked him *why* he had even gotten such a thing, but he'd told her it was free because of a favor he had done for a carnival artist. Some payback, she sniffed.

She and Alice returned to the boarding house. Alice was peeved with her for not encouraging the men's overtures. Rose tried vainly to convince Alice that first impressions were not always what they seemed. Why not wait until tomorrow? If Rick still acted interested in her, then she, Rose, would disappear and let the two have privacy. Whatever was meant to happen, would *happen*. They ate at the local cafeteria, Two Dollar Dinners, and turned in early.

Rose remembers taking a volume of Sherlock Holmes up to bed. The story of *The Red-Headed League* stuck in her mind. Was that it? Yes, that was the one she had read before finally falling to sleep. I must have been really desperate for reading material.

Saturday morning dawned fresh and clear. They had laughed at the breakfast talk of storm rumors. A nor'easter. Alice wanted to shop for a new bathing suit so Rose agreed and they drove to a complex of stores along Atlantic Avenue. Shopping took longer than Rose thought possible but finally Alice emerged from the dressing room wearing what she considered a fairly daring suit. A two-piece, royal blue, with bands of white around the legs and a flat white bow across the bosom. Alice was delighted with her purchase. They picked up milkshakes and fries and ate while driving back to the beach.

The sky was dull pewter when they spread their towels in the same spot as the previous afternoon. It was nearly two in the afternoon. Rose remembered Rick asking if they had eaten and Alice eagerly piping up "No!"

"Then come on with us to Dot's, best crab cakes and cottage fries in town. Our subs are here and we got to grab some food fast." The foursome headed quickly to Dot's, just down the boardwalk, and managed to eat a quick meal in the one remaining booth. Alice had scowled across at Rose when Rick slid in beside her, leaving Reed to eat with Alice. But she lightened up and eventually they *all* teased Reed about the poisonous serpent on his arm. They couldn't have spent more than thirty minutes at Dot's. When they came outside the sky was ominous_— blue-black, threatening rain with each passing second. The wind was picking up.

And then what? The substitute shift raced back to their posts, and Rick and Reed ran to the edge of the water to herd the remaining people in from the ocean. Umbrellas tumbled across the expanse of sand, chairs up-ended, kids' surfboards swirled past. Rose recalled the near hurricane in all directions. Suddenly, Alice shook off her sandals, raced to the water and dived into the crashing waves. This was the first time in two days she had even entered the water; Rose had no idea that Alice could swim. Why this moment?

Rick dived in immediately. She and Reed stood like statues in the surf. She remembered beating on Reed's chest, begging him to go after them, shouting for anybody, somebody, to help her friends. And then all was a blur.

Coming back to the present, Rose hugs the quilt and hears again the pounding of the waves, the beating rain, and the fearful moaning of the wind. If I really did faint, as Reed said I did, then he took me to the one safe place he knew, the lifeguards' shed. That's where the men kept their personal belongings. That's where he became Rick. What did I do when I woke up?

Rose trembles as she retraces the anguishing aftermath of the drowning. Kind strangers had taken her back to the boarding house and notified the police of her friend's disappearance. Reed's clothing, the only remnant of his having worked at Virginia Beach, gave no hint of his identity. Nor of Rick's. The thick wad of bills in his pants pocket totaled nearly five hundred dollars. The police gave that to the beach patrol.

Rose sits up once more. She has total recall now—

breaking the tragic news to Alice's family and driving down dusty one-lane roads to Iris for the funeral. It all became clear to her. Did she write Alice's mother? She hoped she had before her mind had clamped shut on that chapter in her life.

How can the memory of that dreadful brown boarding house be so clear yet no memory of Alice? She was fair. And tall. Beyond that—nothing. And what happened to the volume of Sherlock Holmes I took up to read? Did I return it to the parlor? Why do I even remember such a detail?

Rose sits; chin in hand, pondering all that has transpired this evening. Ellie creeps in and closes the door.

Finally, Ellie asks softly, "Are you all right, Rose?"

"Just fine, Ellie, just fine. I've been wondering if Dot's crab cakes are as good now as they were in 1961."

What Did Rose Mason Read in
Virginia Beach, Virginia in July 1961?

What did I read that night at the beach? Was it *The Red-Headed League*? It may have been Poe, or Dickens. I'm certain it wasn't Shakespeare. Those volumes were too heavy to lift! It's such a petty detail but it nags at me that I can't dredge up the name. How can I visualize that dreary painting of the playful kittens as well as the shelves of old, musty books, but I'm unable to pull the title out of my head? Who's getting old and musty, Rose?

CHAPTER

20

"Post-traumatic stress disorder."

"What's that, Bob?"

Arthur Everett and Bob Lesley have stopped at the elevator. Both men, consumed with their own dark thoughts, have walked silently from Rose's apartment.

Arthur Everett repeats, "What did you say, Bob?"

"Post-traumatic stress disorder. Our lovely Rose has been suffering the pain of this for lo, forty-odd years."

"Sure of that, Doc?"

"As sure as I am that Mr. Conklin is both charlatan and charmer. I don't care if he can bench-press *850 pounds*, the man is trouble."

"But this stress disorder, Bob, does it always affect people the way it did our Rose?"

"No, no, depends on lots of factors — the episode itself, type of victim involved, and the perpetrator of the incident. Some folks go to pieces after being a part of, or being involved in a disaster, and then need long-term psychological help. Some suppress their memories completely, almost a protective amnesia of the brain. As Rose did, apparently. We may never know what happened between Rose and this Conklin fellow, Arthur. In fact, I don't care to know. But something he said or did at dinner unlocked Rose's emotions and all the fears from long ago peaked in her near catatonic reaction. Rose is a survivor, a *strong* survivor, even with her bad hip. I suspect that she wanted us out of there so she could have a showdown with this man and then say good riddance to him. By God, it better be good riddance."

"With Ellie Johnson by her side, I predict that Mr. Conklin will make a rather speedy exit."

"Good night, Arthur. Thanks for your assistance with our favorite invalid."

"And the same to you, Bob. *Ave atque vale.*"

The two men shake hands and continue on their way, Arthur to his bride and Bob Lesley to enjoy a nightcap with Charlie Caldwell and Taki Yokamura.

Paula had been sitting at her desk for so long she has lost track of time. Worry lines crease her striking face and her jaw is clenched.

I shouldn't take the day's work home, she scolds herself. Particularly when home is where I work. But these people are good to me. My role as Resident Director is my *gift* to these seniors, a gift I give with love. I get a boost out of solving the problems that surface here. Usually. But today, Lord, I admit I am whipped. I have so much to figure out.

Perhaps I should accept the Board's offer of a vacation. But where would I go? Without Andre, traveling is not fun. Anyway, how could I leave at this time?

Who is leaving bundles of trash in our hallways? And with burned-out matches. And today's package had charred rags in it. Then there is the professor. Oh, Lord, pray that his plane leaves on time. He's quiet as a mouse, but *so* quiet he's disconcerting. Creeps around in those funny slippers, bowing and looking, looking and bowing. Curious about everything and everybody. And Mrs. McNess. I thought my eyes were playing tricks on me when I saw that man beside her at dinner.

"Okay, girl, you get a grip," she says aloud. "You're lucky to get this job and lucky to be alive in this world. Everything going to look better in the morning. Sun goes down, all the devils come out to worry a body."

Listen to me. I'm lapsing back to child-talk. That means you're lonely and tired. Paula. Time to get some sleep.

She stands and walks to the window. The night outside is black but somehow the emptiness of the sky lifts her spirits. Feeling better about whatever the next day will bring, she switches off the lamp and retires to bed.

ATTENTION ALL RESIDENTS:

Please refer to your Wynfield Hand-
book for complete information on disposal
of trash, recyclables and hazardous materials (pages 9 and 10). Residents who have
any <u>further questions</u> regarding what may
or may not be 'hazardous', please see Ms
Mueller or Mrs. Gallentine.
Thank you.

Paula Gallentine
Resident Director

(EXCERPT FROM *WYNSONG*)

21

Jocey Ribble ducks through the kitchen doorway.

Rick Conklin! He's no good, I just feel it. What does he want with our Mrs. McNess? At least I warned her.

"Hey Jocey, stay and eat with us. Got a couple extra filets and a place with your name on it at the cook's table." Chef Leon beams a 100-watt smile at Jocey as she holds the door for two of the waitresses filing past with trays of steaming food.

"Thanks, Leon, I better not. Mom's expecting me."

"Why not call her from here? We haven't seen you in months. Please, honor us with your presence. Cuisine is exquisite tonight; I have that directly from the Chef." Leon's eyes twinkle at his own joke.

"You know what, Leon? Your offer is too good to pass up. I'll call Mom right now."

Jocey Ribble calls her mother to explain the unexpected invitation. She'll finish about 9:00, lock up the green house and be home around 9:30. Thelma Ribble tells her daughter to have fun. The porch light will be on.

Jocey does have fun. The atmosphere in the Wynfield kitchen is that of easy camaraderie, Chef Leon sees to that. It was tradition for all the *sous chefs*, *salad chefs*, and Marcella, chief of dishwashing detail, to join Leon at the long oak table in the rear of the gleaming kitchen. The wait staff had their own place, closer to the doorway. It was a high compliment to be invited *by* Leon to sit at *his* table. Jocey had been a regular since her early days at Wynfield. She and Leon shared a passion for their respective arts and an easy relationship in which they could discuss their talents easily and without artifice. Earlier, Jocey had wondered if perhaps Leon had asked her to stay for the occasional meal because of a romantic interest. But during three years of breakfasts and dinners, their friendship had remained where it began, flat on the back burner.

Tonight is no different. The two old friends chat about the addition of the Wynfield cottages and the changes they will bring. Jocey worries that the Board might not approve her request for two additional groundskeepers. Leon frets that dinner may have to be served in shifts. It is all business.

Jocey finally leaves the kitchen at 9:00, allowing, at Leon's insistence, Raymond, one of the wait staff to accompany her to the greenhouse door.

"Thanks, Raymond. This was fun tonight, eating with you guys. See you."

Before she goes home, Jocey intends to look around the greenhouse, check on the climate control switches and review work sheets for tomorrow. But a tray of impatiens destined for Montremont Gardens look sickly in the half-light and she decides to give them a shot of plant food.

One of the orchids—*Madame Barrett*—has a bud showing faint color. It begins to unfurl as she watches.

This is going to be a stunner, she thinks. When it finally stopped blooming last year, how many did it have, sixteen blooms on one stem? Spectacular. And here it comes again. Just proves what the right light does! Jocey leans against the potting bench, hands tucked in her overalls' pockets, and peers intently at the willowy orchid.

"You're working mighty late. Paid overtime, are ya?" Jocey jumps a foot.

"How—how did you get in here? What are you *doing* here? I'm locking up right now. You've got to leave." She clutches the keys to her truck and starts for the greenhouse door.

"I'm not leaving. *We're* leaving! Gimme them keys!" Reed Chenowski wrenches the keys from Jocey's hand with such force that it catches her right index finger. She cries out.

"That hurt? Just wait. Come on, you gotta drive us out of here."

Jocey's hand does hurt, but she sizes up her visitor and instinctively knows that she must not show weakness. How can I stall him? How can I signal Leon or Raymond?

"Why are you still here? Did you see Mrs. McNess? Isn't she the one you came to see?"

"Shut up!" he cries, slapping her hard across her left cheek. "You're going to get me out of here. You get your sweet ass in that driver's seat and we're going to roll away from Wynfield Farms like you and me's on a date. And we are. I've had my eyes on you from the day we had lunch."

Her cheek is chafing from the blow. Jocey is incensed and smarts from the memory of that lunch.

"I said get in and drive. I'll tell you where to go. Just get in. *Now.*"

Too frightened to utter another word, Jocey obeys. Reed loosens his tie, then takes it off altogether. He rolls down the window and flings it into the night.

"Won't be needing a tie again soon. No sense in trying to impress a lady who won't be impressed. How 'bout you? Are you impressed with me?"

Jocey's heart beats wildly. Can he see it going *thud-thud-thud* in her chest? What have I read in newspapers about women getting kidnapped? Keep them talking, keep them thinking about themselves, never act like you're afraid? Oh God, help me, please!

"Where shall I drive?" she asks as she pulls onto one secondary road.

"Anywhere. Not in town. How much gas you got?"

"Enough," Jocey replies, cursing herself for filling the gas tank this morning.

"O.K. Let's go to Virginia Beach."

"Virginia Beach? Are you crazy?" she yells. "That's six to eight hours from here. I'm not driving to Virginia Beach. Besides, I don't know how to get there."

Jocey startles herself with this outburst. She has no idea of how to reach the coast and she is terrified at the prospect of trying to find it in the middle of the night with a maniac beside her.

"I said we're going to Virginia Beach and *that* is where we're going."

Jocey feels Rick's finger poking into her ribs and starts to brush his hand away. She freezes. Even in the dim dashboard light, she can see the snub nose of a small gun.

Once again, a voice from someone inside her, someone she'd never known, says, "Get your gun out of my ribs. Please."

I will not plead. I will be firm and polite.

"*Now* Mr. Conklin."

"Just as long as you know the score. I'll keep this handy, though. Chenowski, that's my name. Reed Chenowski."

"But you said the other day...it was Conklin. Rick Conklin."

"I told you wrong. Live around here?"

"Yes. Not far from Wynfield Farms. Oh, God—" Jocey suddenly remembers telling her mother she'd be home around 9:30, tops. They'll worry. Call the office, perhaps.

"What the matter?"

"Mom is going to expect me home soon. If I don't show up, she'll worry herself to death."

"Nah, she'll think you're on a hot date. Don't you ever go on hot dates, Jocelyn?"

Jocey hates the way he drags out her name, making the two syllables sound like three.

I won't tell him to call me Jocey. I won't. And I won't tell him I don't date. What would he do to me then? For a moment, Jocey loses her cool demeanor. She breathes deeply, gulps again, and announces combatively, "Of course I date.

But my father has cancer and I don't keep them up late. My parents need their sleep and I help when I get home. Change my dad's position in bed, give him medication, you know."

"No, I wouldn't know. My old man's been dead to me for over fifty years. Mom, too. Both of them, flat-out dead."

"Is that why you're so bitter?"

"Don't try to change the subject. Where are we now? We still headed for Virginia Beach?"

Jocey has been driving through back roads of Botetourt County. She figures the longer she takes to reach the interstate, the more gas she'll use and the sooner she'll have to stop. She is leaving Wildcat Hollow and knows exactly how many miles it is before I-81.

"I'm trying to get my bearings. There's not a direct way to reach the interstate from Wynfield. But we're coming to an exit. Then do I go north or south?"

"North. I know that much. We go north towards Charlottesville, then get on I-64. Somewhere along the way we pickup the route to the beach. A lot's changed in the forty years since I was there. Whole interstate is new."

Jocey's mind whirls. Maybe I can get him to talk so much he'll get sleepy and then I can turn around without him realizing it.

"Tell me about it. I wasn't even born then."

"Joc-e-lyn, I was the best damned lifeguard at Virginia Beach in the summer of 1961."

"Did you save lots of lives?"

"Shut up! Did you talk to Rose Mason?"

Jocey is stunned but merely asks, "Who's Rose Mason?"

"The McNess dame. I told you when *I* met her she was Rose *Mason*."

"You met Mrs. McNess at Virginia Beach in 1961? And you've come all the way down from Detroit to look her up?"

"Correct, Miss Prissy Britches. Think I'm pretty hot, huh?"

"Take your hand away from my knee or I'm stopping right now. And I mean it."

Oh, God, let me sound tough, Jocey prays. To her surprise, Reed removes his hand and seemed to shrink against the door.

"Tell me about meeting Mrs. McNess," Jocey requests in a voice as mellow as honey in a hive.

"She was the prettiest woman I'd ever seen. Down at the beach for three days. Classy, she was. Came down with a dog of a friend. We were about to have a really good time when—"

"What happened? Would I know her friend? Sounds exciting. What did you do?"

"Don't wanna talk about it. Terrible storm. Worst nor'easter to hit Virginia Beach in thirty years. Never saw Rose again."

"What is her friend's name?"

Jocey's question is rewarded with the blessed sound of silence, followed by deep, ratcheting snoring.

Now's my chance! Oh God, where can I turn? How do I get back to the southbound lane? There. Right ahead—a crossover.

Jocey carefully navigates the truck across the median strip and over the chain that is mercifully resting on the ground. There is a God, she thinks. She quickly heads south and toward the gas station. Surely they are open; maybe even a state trooper stopping in for coffee. He would help!

Suddenly her passenger bolts up in his seat and cries, "Where the hell are we going? Did you turn around back there?"

"I turned only because my oil is low and I'm not ruining my truck because of your crazy ideas. I'll stop and get a quart of oil and then we can go on. Don't worry, we haven't lost many miles."

"You better be telling me the truth, Prissy Britches. You know what's in my pocket."

Oh, do I ever, panics Jocey. Just about twelve inches away from me. Oh, God, let Clem Atkinson be on duty tonight. Please God—let Clem be there.

Jocey pulls into the Mobil apron and is turning off the

ignition when Reed suddenly barks, "Not here. Pull over there, by the air pump. Don't park in the light."

She does not argue and drives to the far side of the lot. "May I go in and get my oil?" she asks petulantly.

"Sure. Only no funny business, right?"

Jocey has not thought out the details of her plan. She knows only that it is imperative to alert someone to her plight. The sooner the authorities know, the quicker this whole mess will be over.

"Clem?" she calls, walking into the high-voltage lights of the Mobil station.

"Clem's not here tonight. Whatya want?" This from a tall, skinny blonde teenager in need of a shave. The name embroidered over his left shirt pocket identifies him as 'Jerry'.

"I—I need a quart of oil. And help!" She thrusts the quart of oil toward the clerk. Through the glass, Jocey sees Reed jumping out of the truck and following her into the store.

"Help?" Jerry asks, puzzling over this interruption to the television program he had been watching.

"I'm being kidnapped. Please help me! Call the police!"

Jerry looks up as Reed saunters casually through the door. "My wife bothering you fellow?" he asks pleasantly, then laughs loudly at his own joke.

The imperceptible click behind him is lost in the volume of Reed's forced laugh.

"Nah, not bothering me. She just say's she's being kidnapped. That's rich, a good one for my supervisor in the morning."

Reed's right hand reaches into his pocket and grabs his snub-nosed friend.

Bang!

Jerry's mouth still gapes in a half-smirk. His eyes close. Blood spurts from the green shirt as cardboard knees crumple and he hits the floor.

"He ain't going to tell his super *anything* in the morning. Come on, we gotta run."

"You killed him. You killed an innocent man, right in front of me. I can't drive. I'm too upset. I just can't—"

The television in the corner continues to blare.

"Oh yes you can. And you will. You're a part of this now. You and me. Police'll think robbery and they suspect a woman every time. Get in."

"What about the oil? My truck will be ruined. We need that oil."

"Your oil is fine. Why d'ya think I got out? We'll get further down the highway, stop for gas, and check it again. I snatched some doughnuts from Jerry there so we have some food. Drive, woman, drive."

Jocey follows orders. Civility vanished at the Mobil station with the blast that killed Jerry. She tries not to think of the decent man lying on the floor, bleeding to death because of the creep beside her. When will he turn the gun on her? She weighs her options.

Would I rather be killed out right, like Jerry, without a chance to beg or run? Or would I rather be raped and tortured and have horrible things done to me and left for dead? Jocey shivers. No question: I'll take death.

"What do you think Mrs. McNess will say when this comes out in the paper? Two killings in one night."

"What do you mean, *two* killings?"

"Why me, of course. I'll be useless to you once we stop. And you know what? I'm not afraid to die. I'll stop right here if you want to shoot me."

"Will you shut up? You're my ticket to freedom. Rose and her old lady friends will vouch for my good behavior. Nice personality and all that bull. It's you that went berserk. Grabbed my gun, shot the guy in the gas station and forced me to come along on a joy ride. Said you'd never seen the ocean and why not tonight? It's you against me, baby, you against me."

Would the police believe this twisted tale? If he fooled Mrs. McNess, he sure could convince just about anybody. I might be about to die but I'm *not* going to pull over and let him shoot me like a dog. Who would look after Mom and Dad?

Jocey feels numb, exhausted, all but paralyzed by the fear that is settling in her bones. It is nearly midnight. At least six hours driving before Virginia Beach.

JOCELYN RIBBLE'S CONVERSATION WITH GOD

O dear God, what have I gotten myself into? God, can you hear me? I pray that you'll let me live, please, please let me live. Mom and Dad need me so much, they depend on me. Please, please let me live. Please don't let this Rick person, Reed, whoever he is, harm me. Not, *You* know, rape me or do what he tried to do at lunch last week. Damn! Why did I agree to have lunch with him? That started everything. *Everything.* If I hadn't gone to lunch, he wouldn't even know me, and I wouldn't be here right now, driving to someplace I've never seen and don't know how to get to. Damn my ignorant self. But I'm here and unless I wreck my truck I'm stuck until I see a cop or something. I've got to act like I'm in control. Strong, Jocey, strong. Try to sing. Sing? *Sing?* I'm too scared to do anything but pray. And listen. What is he babbling about now? Carnival. I'm tired of hearing about the carnival. Dear God, are You listening to me? I swear I've been a good person, don't let him kill me like he did poor Jerry. Oh God, help Jerry, help Mom and Dad, help *ME!*

CHAPTER

22

"Jocey is missing? Say that again, Mrs. G. Missing, you say? How did you ... Yes, yes, of course I shall. Yes ... we'll be down as soon as I get some coffee in her. Thank you for letting us know. No, no of course I won't call anyone else."

Rose is fuzzyheaded and disoriented after a night of solid sleep. She is almost too rested, as if she were floating, floating weightlessly along on that endless river once again. That voice? Is it Ellie? Of course. Ellie has spent the night, and is making the coffee she smells. But who's Ellie talking to?

"Rose!" Ellie plunges into the bedroom, voice and vitality shattering any semblance of lingering sleep Rose may harbor.

"Rose, honey, I hate to wake you like this but the most awful thing has happened. Did you hear the phone just now?"

"Just some talking, Ellie. Tell me ..."

"I grabbed it on the first ring, thinking it was *him* and I was going to fix his wagon. But Rose, it was Mrs. G. and she said—Jocey is missing!"

Rose struggles to sit up. She rubs her eyes and asks, "Jocey is missing? That can't be! Oh, Ellie, we have to do something. I must get dressed, go help Mrs. Gallentine and see—"

"That's what I'm about to tell you! She wants you down in her office P.D.Q. The Sheriff is on his way to ask some questions. Mrs. G. said she wants you there because you know Jocey so well. What is it Rose? You have the strangest look on your face."

Rose McNess is replaying Jocey's late-night visit and her description of Mr. Rick Conklin. 'Smarmy.' Could Jocey have possibly gone off with the man? I'm not the brightest match in the box in the early morning, but I'm beginning to sense a devious plan.

"Strange look you say?"

"Yes, *very* strange, as if a winning lottery number just flashed across your screen."

"Merely putting two and two together, Ellie, and I'm afraid it adds up to one thing — trouble. Let's get dressed and go down to the office."

ELLIE JOHNSON WRITES IT BOLD
AND IN GOLD

I'll write fast while Rose is getting dressed. Something tells me this is BIG trouble for our prim little horticulturist. Poor girl! Why are the victims always the good girls? And why am I so sure that Reed so and so is involved in her disappearance? And why is Rose so mysterious? She knows more than she is letting on, almost as if she has been Mother Confessor for Jocey Ribble. Could she? Anything is possible. Wow. Only been at Wynfield a little more than two years and I could write a book about all that goes on here. Oops-got to run. Hear Rose at her door now. More later.

CHAPTER

23

"Mrs. Rose McNess, Sheriff Hershberger. Sheriff, Mrs. Rose McNess, the resident we spoke about this morning."

"Miz McNess, we meet again! How'do! Why, we're practically old friends, Miz Gallentine. Sorry I didn't catch the name when we talked early on. Blaster was going in the background. All hell's breakin' loose with that shooting down in Daleville last night. Sorry, ladies, you'll have to forgive my language."

"Then you *know* Mrs. McNess?" glancing from one to the other, Mrs. Gallentine states this more as a matter of fact than a possibility.

"Sheriff Hershberger was kind enough to help two years ago when we had a missing person case."

"Ah ha," said Mrs. Gallentine, "the Rector woman, I suppose."

"Yes, sadly, but—how did you—?"

Mrs. Gallentine's arched eyebrows tell Rose in an instant that the departing Miss Moss took great delight in regaling her with the deeds and misdeeds of the Wynfield residents.

The portly sheriff sits down heavily and pulls a small black spiral notebook from his shirt pocket. His TUMS are in the other pocket; never know when he might need one. Looking squarely at Rose he says sternly, "Tell me what you know about this mystery man the Ribble girl may have taken off with."

Rose is distraught. She thinks she may faint. Wouldn't that be the icing on the cake? I promised Jocey that her lunch date was our secret. How does the sheriff know about him? How did he connect the three of us?

Mrs. Gallentine leans across and in a low voice confides, "I told the sheriff what you told me about Jocey meeting your friend in the garden the other day."

"And Jocey's mother, Mrs. Thelma Ribble, good woman, known her all m'life. Having a hard time right now with Jocey's dad. Thelma told me this morning when she called that Jocey thinks this fellow must be okay if he's come all the way to Virginia to visit *you.*" Apparently Jocey confided something to Thelma. He leans across to Rose and stares blankly at her face.

The sheriff's cell phone rings, stopping the questions and the staring.

"Yeah, Hershberger here. Withers? Thanks for checking in. How's the victim? That's good. Intensive care, huh. Yeah. Yeah. Any prints? Well, damn it to hell, man, check again. What about the witness? Did you get a'hold of him? Good, good, you got that part right, anyway. I'll be back in the office in ten minutes."

Sheriff Hershberger punches the phone off and returns it to his hip pocket. This maneuver is an awkward isometric exercise, one more indication that Sheriff Hershberger's girth is an encumbrance he could do without. He pops a TUMS into his mouth, shakes his head, and again apologizes for his profanity.

Rose worries less about the sheriff's profanity than she does his blood pressure. His beefy face reddened visibly during the phone conversation and he is beginning to sweat. Droplets the size of Malaga grapes form on his temple. Forgetting for a moment the real purpose of this meeting—finding Jocey Ribble—Rose pulls a clean linen handkerchief from her pocket and presses it into the sheriff's hand. He automatically wipes his broad forehead before the grapes fall onto his notebook.

"Sorry about that call, ladies. Got a shooting victim who's going to make it, thank God. Lucky guy, bullet clean through his right shoulder. Other side, be another story. And we got a witness. Now, where was I?"

Rose recounts what she knows about Reed's background (not much), the fact that he came south from Detroit (he says) and how they are associated (however that may be construed).

"This man is passing through Fincastle, Miz McNess and looks you up? That is pretty thin. Few people just *happen* to pass through Fincastle. And fewer still end up here in Wynfield Farms."

This overstuffed officer, thinks Rose, is more clever than he appears.

"Sheriff Hershberger, Mrs. Gallentine, I am not proud of what I am getting ready to say. But I feel I must if it concerns Jocey. We've barely mentioned her this morning and I'm worried sick about her."

"Indirectly, Mrs. McNess, everything we're talking about here relates to Jocey Ribble's disappearance. We have an excellent profile on that young lady and there's no way on God's green earth she'd walk away *unless* she was forced. Ninety-nine cases out of a hundred, woman gets into a car with someone she knows. Or has met. Now, please tell us what you were about to say. *All* confidential, by the way. Even my notes."

Rose begins and tells about the Virginia Beach weekend with Alice, the storm, the drowning, and the stolen identity. With lowered voice she adds, "He told me last night that he never got over his feelings for me. It was puppy-love palaver you'd expect from a teenager, certainly not a man in his sixties."

"And what did you have to say to that?" asks the sheriff.

"The truth. I never had any feelings for that man. Ironically, I had never given that tragic weekend or Reed another thought. That episode was in deep freeze in my brain. Until last evening, when everything came pouring out. A real thaw. I remembered *when* and *where* I had known Reed Chenowski."

"How do you feel about Mr. Chenowski now?"

"He is still a coward, Sheriff. He didn't try to save my friend nor his colleague and then compounded that by stealing his friend's good name."

"Do you think he is capable of abducting Jocey Ribble?"

"I will have to answer 'yes' to that, Sheriff. He tries too hard to be something he is not. Too slick, too cool. Is he violent? I don't know. Jocey told me she didn't like him when she met him in the garden, and said he had 'steely eyes'."

I will not tell a white lie about Jocey going to lunch with Reed. We've passed that point. Why did I give my one handkerchief to the Sheriff? Now I think *I'm* starting to perspire.

"And how about you, Mrs. Gallentine? You told me you'd met the man. What's your opinion?"

"I saw him with Mrs. McNess but she did not, as I recall, formally introduce us. My opinion? For what it is worth, I think the man is capable of anything."

"Either of you add any identifying features? Mrs. Gallentine here filled me in with specific physical data. Say, happen to have a picture of this man, Miz McNess? Otherwise our sketch artist will go to work..."

"Pictures? Of course not!" Rose spit out vehemently. "I'm sorry, I've about had it with Mr. Chenowski!"

Why *would* I have a picture of someone I barely knew, and have not thought about in over forty years? Sounds like a question *he* would ask: 'Don't you have a picture of me at Virginia Beach?' Ha! Rose is embarrassed by her outburst. She studies the crown molding, the books on the shelves, Paula's tidy desk. She looks anywhere to avoid the mournful basset hound face of Sheriff Hershberger. Both the resident director and the sheriff sit, waiting.

"No additional details then?" the lawman asks in a softer tone.

"The tattoo!" Rose remembers, and almost screams as she does, "The blue snake! Reed Chenowski has a horrible blue snake twisting around his left wrist. That will positively identify him—there can't be two tattoos like that in the world."

"Great, Miz McNess." Sheriff Hershberger stands, his broad frame filling the space and sucking all air from the small office. "I better get back and process these facts. Thanks for your time, ladies. Good to see you again, Miz McNess. Now don't either of you worry. We'll get Jocey Ribble back here in no time. Got patrols blanketing the state, checking on her license number and truck model. She won't get far."

"Virginia Beach!"

"What?" asks the sheriff, pausing at the door.

"He's taking Jocey to Virginia Beach! Reed Chenowski is obsessed with his role as lifeguard. He's going back to the place where it all began. And in a way, where he ended the life he might have had. Sheriff, try Virginia Beach. Please. Trust my instincts."

"On it now." Rose and Paula's last glimpse of Sheriff Hershberger is one of his grappling with the cell phone as he lumbers down the steps to his waiting car.

"Well, Mrs. McNess," states Resident Director Gallentine in her crisp, efficient managerial voice, "I think that went very well. In a curious manner, Sheriff Hershberger inspires confidence. He'll get *my* vote in the November elections."

"Only if he brings Jocey back," cries Rose. "I am responsible for all of this. If I had not had surgery, if Jocey hadn't been where she was, if my past hadn't come calling—"

"Stop that right now, Rose McNess. There is no way I'm going to let you shoulder the blame for what has happened. Be rational, woman! We don't even know if your visitor is the man who abducted Jocey, or truthfully, *if* she is abducted. Coincidences happen. This may be a case of several coincidences colliding. You are feeling less then your regular self because of major surgery. Shh! Don't interrupt me," she said when Rose looked as if she were going to speak. "I've seen women your age go through the same procedure and they always wake up wondering when the truck hit them. I predict, Rose McNess, that as soon as you toss that walker away you'll be operating at full tilt." She smiles at Rose. "End of lecture. I better get moving. Would you look at the time! It's11:00 and Romero will be taking Professor Yokamura to the airport."

"You're wonderful, Paula Gallentine," Rose says quietly, touching the woman's arm. "You've made me feel so much better. Look, Ellie and Taki are coming now."

Professor Yokamura bows deeply and extends his hand to each. The tears in his large, sad eyes speak the volumes he is incapable of saying. There is no language barrier for gratitude.

After more bowing to Frances Keynes-Livingston, Father Charlie, and the gathering of residents in the Reception Hall, Romero finally persuades the professor that the car is waiting and the road to the Roanoke airport is long.

They stand on the steps and wave until Taki's white handkerchief disappears in the distance.

"Farewell, Taki, farewell one more grand adventure. We're all going to miss our Japanese ambassador of everything."

"What good company he is," laments a genuinely crestfallen Frances.

"I'll second that. Why don't we all go down to the pub and have a cup of coffee. It will cheer us up, Besides, I'm dying to know what's going on, Rose. I was careful to keep all of this from Taki. I saw no need to spoil his last hour with us. Now how about that coffee?" Ellie's face is bright with anticipation.

They settle at a corner table and order coffee and scones. Frances and Ellie press close to Rose, waiting expectantly. Rose tells her friends as much as she can remember of the hour with Sheriff Hershberger.

"Does he think it *is* a kidnapping?" implores Frances.

"Come to think of it, the word kidnapping was never used. He called it an 'abduction' several times, but never kidnapping. A matter of semantics, I would say. The sheriff seems convinced that mysterious Mr. Chenowski is the abductor." Rose stops, clearly reflecting on her hour in Mrs.

Gallentine's office and the statements she made.

"Somehow, in my heart, I don't want to believe Reed Chenowski is capable of violence or evil. After all, he did come to see me in good faith, to profess worthwhile feelings. What do you think, Ellie?"

"I think your reputation as a sex kitten lured him here," Ellie jokes. They roar at this, none more than Rose.

"Seriously, sweetie," Ellie continues, "I think your naiveté is showing. You said yourself he was a coward forty years ago and a dishonest coward at that. I have to say that I am in the sheriff's camp when he points the finger at Reed."

"I *knew* you were going to say that, Ellie! I admit I'm gullible and softhearted. One more question, do you think I should call Mrs. Ribble and explain why..."

"No!" came the immediate interruption, to Rose's immense relief.

"Let me pass on a piece of good news I've picked up," whispers Frances, dunking the last of a cranberry scone in her coffee and then nibbling delicately.

"There is some good news? Speak up," begs Rose.

"Leon the chef has been secretly pining for Jocey for three years. It seems Jocey slips into the kitchen for her evening meal with some regularity, at Leon's behest, of course. The man is mad about her! When he heard about her disappearance, he drove straight over to the Ribble's to offer his sympathy.

"And," continues the Bryn Mawr doyenne, "Mrs. Ribble greets Leon as if he were Jocey's best friend. Said she had heard all about him from her daughter, how wonderful he has been, *et cetera, et cetera.* Seems our Jocey also has been hiding *her* secret feelings for Leon these three years."

"Bravo, Frances. If only they find Jocey and bring her back safely," Rose offers. "No one loves a happy ending any more than I do. We're dangling over the edge of a cliff, hanging on by our fingernails until we see Jocey drive up."

Ellie happens to glance toward the door and spots Mrs. Gallentine peering into the pub. "Look who's here! Come join us, Mrs. G."

"Rose," whispers Mrs. Gallentine, "I must see you."

"Please, say whatever you have to say, Mrs. Gallentine. Everyone knows about Jocey's disappearance and nothing is going to be secret very long. What now?"

"I'm frantic! Sheriff Hershberger just called. Remember the shooting in Daleville last night? It seems Jocey's fingerprints have been found at the scene of the crime."

"What!"

The three faces around the table mirror Mrs. Gallentine's expression; shock, horror, and disbelief.

"They were found on a quart of oil sitting on the counter at the Mobil station. I hope this doesn't make them think that *Jocey* shot the attendant!"

Sheriff Adam Niblock* Hershberger
Takes Measure of Mrs. Rose McNess

This little lady is a tough cookie. Remember her from the Rector drowning case. When was that? Two years ago? 'Bout that, at least. 'Member she and her dog led the deputy down to the lake. Sergeant Connell said she never hesitated touching the body, not even backing off when he pulled it from the water. Guts. She's got guts. But she's not puttin' all her cards on the table in this poker game. Knows more about the Ribble gal than she's willing to spill. I'll get it out of her. She's got a steel backbone but I'll get it to bend, new hip or not. Think this new Director senses it too. Like the looks of that lady. Beats the heck out of old what's-her-name Moss.

* "His Nibs" behind his back by all fellow officers and underlings in the Sheriff's Department.

"I bet they do suspect her," cries Ellie. "That explains the sheriff's deputies in the greenhouse this morning."

"How do you know *that*, Mrs. Johnson?" questions Mrs. Gallentine.

"I thought I'd left my glasses case down there when we worked on the flowers. I discovered it was missing so I slipped down before we met Taki. Four deputies were dusting for prints and putting some of Jocey's tools in plastic bags. They were looking for a clean set of Jocey's fingerprints!"

"You're exactly right, Ellie. They must have matched a set of her prints with ones they found in Daleville. But Jocey pull the trigger of a gun? Impossible! And what about the witness the sheriff mentioned? You remember, Mrs. Gallentine, when the sheriff took the call and he asked about the witness. That will clear Jocey," Rose bursts out passionately, adamantly. She looks around, expecting nods of agreement from her friends and the Resident Director. The three sit motionless, their faces blank.

Mrs. Gallentine speaks first. "Perhaps they were looking for the man's prints, or checking for signs of a struggle."

The women all nod in agreement. "Yes, that's a possibility," Rose says. "I don't want to think that anyone would suspect Jocey."

There was another pause, then Frances stands. "I must

be going," She pats Rose on the arm and thanks Ellie.

"We should go too, Rose. Ready?" Ellie looks at her friend.

"I'll call you if—and when—I hear anything at all, Mrs. McNess," Mrs. Gallentine murmurs solicitously.

Ellie and Rose sleepwalk to the elevator, no words passing between them. Approaching their apartments, Ellie asks, "Won't you come in, Rose? I've got a comfortable chair with your name on it."

"Thanks, Ellie, but I feel awful. I think I should call Mrs. Ribble. Indirectly I *am* responsible for all that has happened."

"For goodness sakes don't tell her that. You'll be carrying a sack of guilt like a snail carries a shell. But do whatever you think right. You will, anyway. Have you given a thought to dinner this evening? You've got to eat. Keep up your strength and all."

"I know, I know, Ellie. You sound like one of my children. I have no appetite at the moment. Let me give you a ring later."

They blow kisses across the hallway and retreat to their respective nests.

Rose tries to fathom how her world has turned upside down in the past twenty-four hours. She wonders what she will say to Mrs. Ribble, or rather what she *should* say to Mrs. Ribble.

'I'm sorry Jocey's been abducted by an acquaintance of mine.'

Should I call Annie? Why worry her unnecessarily? There is not one thing that anyone can do that is not already being done. I just pray that the police find that pair before they reach Virginia Beach.

Rose spreads the telephone book open on her kitchen table and is looking through it when someone knocks. An insistent knock demanding instant attention.

"Come in!" She continues her search for *Ribble, Kenneth.*

"Disturbing your lunch, Mrs. McNess?" Chef Leon

stands in her doorway.

"Chef Leon," she exclaims. "You're not disturbing anything. This is an honor. Do come in."

"Looks as if you are making some calls. Shall I come back?"

"No indeed, Leon. In fact, you can help me. I must call Jocey's mother. Would you mind looking up the Ribble's number? These old tired eyes just can't find it."

"No need to look it up, Mrs. McNess. That's why I came, to talk about Jocey. I just called her mother. Here's the number." He pulls a small slip of paper from his pocket and slides it across the table to Rose.

"I don't know what to do, Mrs. McNess. Her mother is weeping and the entire family is hysterical. One of Jocey's sisters told me they were all wild with worry. I can't blame them. What can I do?"

"What can any of us do, Leon? I never realized until now that you care about Jocey. Deeply care, I mean. Correct?"

"Oh, God, yes, Mrs. McNess. For three years now. I've been patiently waiting and hoping that she'd see it. I know she likes me. We have fun whenever she eats with us. But neither of us has gotten up the courage to speak of anything like *a date*. And I hate myself now. Look what I may have lost."

The young chef perched on the edge of the kitchen table is a picture of melancholy. Leon has not shaved today, and his dark beard, furrowed with worry lines, adds years to his countenance.

"I don't want to hear that, Leon. I firmly believe that Jocey will be found, soon, and will be back before the day is over. Furthermore, I believe she is safe. Unharmed. I have complete faith in what I am saying."

"Oh, that I could believe you, Mrs. McNess."

"You better believe me, Leon. Now, you asked me what you can do? I'm going to *tell* you what you can do."

"Anything, Mrs. McNess. Say the word."

"First, either concoct something delicious or pull something out of your freezer and deliver it to the Ribble household. Food always says comfort when our tongues fail. You know the good old Southern tradition of bringing food in time of tragedy."

"I can easily do that. Anything else?"

"Absolutely. In light of all the commotion today, I think the residents would appreciate a simple buffet this evening. Nothing fancy, no serving at the tables. Leftovers or whatever is easiest. Let folks take pot luck."

"That sure would make my life simpler, Mrs. McNess. Hard to focus on cooking right now. Think Mrs. Gallentine would approve? She runs a pretty tight ship as far as the dining room is concerned."

"I'll call her. It is our *joint* decision."

"You're something, Mrs. McNess. When you set your mind on something, you get it done. You *do* think Jocey is going to be safe? The suspect isn't the guy you had in for dinner last evening, is it? Is he a decent man?"

Rose shakes her head sadly and repeats some of what she had told the sheriff. "The Greeks have a word for his problem, Leon. *Hubris,* which means overwhelming pride or presumption."

"God, I hate him. If he harms Jocey in any way—"

"Jocey is no dummy, Leon. I'm willing to bet she outsmarts Mr. Chenowski. We just have to wait and see how long it takes her."

"Thanks, Mrs. McNess. I'd appreciate you not saying anything about my feelings for Jocey. I don't want to spring anything on her too soon."

"Don't be an idiot, Leon! I wouldn't advise waiting. In fact, I suggest you tell her the minute she returns. You don't want her slipping out of your fingers!"

The young man waves and lopes down the corridor, causing Rose to wonder, not for the first time, why good cooks always look as if they never ate anything they prepare.

Rose dials the Ribble household, only to be told what Leon had reported. She asks Jocey's sister to convey her sympathy to Thelma Ribble.

Wynfield Farms' evening meal is hardly the subdued affair Rose proposed. Chef Leon and his staff had prepared a dazzling array of specialties. The residents, not at all disappointed at the lack of a formal dinner, were in high, if not exactly festive, spirits.

Change is good, Rose affirms. A break in the routine takes folks out of their comfortable ruts. Given a choice, we'll choose the safe trail every day. Besides, the buffet gives some of the staff a well-deserved night on the town. I wonder if the younger ones go to the same spot in Fincastle where Jocey and Reed ate lunch? What was it, the *Skipjack, Skipperjack, Skipper Jack's?* Well that's hardly germane now.

There is congenial conversation, jocular give and take throughout the dining room. By tacit understanding, no one mentions Reed nor Jocey. The Everetts busy themselves with second helpings of scalloped oysters. Father Charlie and Frances return twice for fresh asparagus and Ellie laughs that she is turning into a pudding—corn pudding, to be precise.

Time passes swiftly. The meal is pleasant and uncomplicated. Each of Rose's friends wonders if perhaps they might have imagined the Chenowski affair. Was it really just *last* evening?

Dessert is enjoyed, coffee is sipped and chairs are pushed back. Sentiments—"Good night, see you tomorrow, sleep tight!" float across the dining tables as seniors head for their apartments.

"I think we deserve a nightcap, don't you Bob?" asks Albert Warrington, looking at Rose, the Everetts, Bob Lesley, and others assembled nearby. "My treat. I never seem to see you good people any more. Will you join me in the pub?"

"That's the price you pay for getting too famous for us," joshes Bob Lesley.

"Agreed!" Arthur chimes in enthusiastically. "Your skill and talents have elevated you to the ranks of the elite. Deservedly so, I add. Lib and I read the recent headline in the *Washington Post.* The one about your speaking on latest techniques in taxidermy. Where was that, Albert? The Smithsonian?"

"Correct, Arthur. They were desperate for a speaker. But will you or will you not join me for a nightcap? Remember, my treat."

"Sure," the crowd agrees. "No telling when you'll make this offer again!"

"Rose, do you feel like staying?" Ellie whispers.

"I do, Ellie. I feel strangely up tonight. Nervous energy, I guess. Let's join the group. As Arthur says, we never see Albert anymore. After all that has transpired in the last twenty-four hours, this is very welcome."

"Ten minutes, Rose. Twenty at the max. And I'll be a martinet tonight." Ellie manages to scowl severely.

At *The Rose and The Grape,* Albert orders club soda for Rose and brandies for everyone else.

"Rose, you look pleased with yourself this evening. A sea change, I must say, after the debacle of last night and this morning." Charlie Caldwell does not mince words.

"I am feeling pleased, Charlie, but not with myself. My *personal* self, I mean. I am worried sick about Jocey but my faith is intact. I just believe that life turns out far better than we have any right to expect. I've had a few past experiences that have seasoned my philosophy. I'm going to keep on looking at the glass half full. With my lucky talisman—"

As if he were waiting for the words "lucky talisman" Professor Yokamura pokes his head around the pub door and says in his soft voice, "Pardon."

They turn as one, dumbfounded to see the professor. Slowly, surprised expressions give way to smiles and exclamations of pleasure. Several of the men rise and grasp his hand.

"Taki! You're supposed to be halfway to California. What in the world happened?" Ellie is grinning from ear to ear and poised to embrace the shy, slight man.

"Yes, tell us all!" several people say at once.

"Give him a chance, folks. I think the professor is trying," chides Charlie Caldwell

"What do you call it? A wild beast hit? Romero takes me to airport. Romero leaves. I wait. And wait. Then Mr. USAirways tells me there is a wild beast hit and no planes today in Roanoke, Virginia."

"A strike! That's what he means: A strike in the airlines. Say, that's a darn good description, Taki, 'wild beast hit.' Better than 'strike' if you ask me." Arthur Everett takes obvious delight in the professor's translation.

"Ah. Str-ike. I try it: *strike.* Yes, that is what happens. So I wait, then I ask Taki, 'Do you wish to return to Tokyo? Traffic on all sides? People crowding in waves on subway and streets? Air thick with smoke and engine fumes? Nowhere to say prayers or look at flowers?' Taki answers: '*No,* I do not return to Tokyo. I wish to remain at Wynfield Farms and complete research here.' I call Head Prefect at Tokyo University. I wait and wait but I get him in sleep. I explain what I will do. He says 'Good, Taki. Goodnight, Taki.' So, here I am. Many dollars for taxicab to Wynfield Farms. Must speak to Mrs. Gallentine this night."

"Hooray! By God, Taki, you made the right decision! I'm proud of you. Sure, stay here at Wynfield Farms. I'll go with you to see Mrs. Gallentine. Dollars to doughnuts she'll be delighted. Sit down and join us in a brandy. You need it after such a day." Father Charlie beams at Taki with almost paternal affection.

The residents chat happily and wonder if Mrs. Gallentine *will* be as pleased as they are with Taki's return.

"We'll get you a position as visiting scholar, Taki. I'm sure my secondary school associates will be delighted to have you speak to their humanity classes. You'll be so busy you won't have time to miss the old country," preens Arthur.

"My desire is to keep busy. I wish to try some paintings of the famous Wynfield gardens. It is beautiful here." The man with sad eyes looks happy at the prospect of unexpected time with his new friends.

"We'll look forward to showing you a glorious Botetourt County summer, Taki," says Bob Lesley, ever gracious to his guest. "Look how the days are already growing longer. The sky is still bright as noon out there. Why, that's not daylight! My God, that's a fire! The cottages are on fire!"

Odell Stroup Reflects On Witnessing A Crime

Why in tarnation the sheriff wants to keep me here is more'n I can figure. Gave 'em my story, even if I was a mite late in getting' there. Gave it to both him *and* the idiot he sent to question me. Can't they understand when a man's got to piss he's got to piss? Had to stop at Mobil for a tank of gas anyway. My fault it got dark on me. Auction over in Rocky Mount went on too long, danged caller an idiot, too. Don't like night drivin'. Told the Sheriff that; not safe for Odell drivin' home to Eagle Rock at night. I got to go back and collect them cows I bought. When's he goin' to let me go and collect m' cows? Told him about pickin' up that fellow with the tattoo, two, three days before this shootin'. Right shifty I tells myself then. Off to see someone in Wynfield Farms. Hmmph. Probably off to see about a job. Shoulda sent him down to the Roanoke market. He coulda been a bean picker with no trouble. Get a job right off the bat. I sure as hell didn't want him on my land. Shifty blue eyes. Yep, I 'member that about him. Saw him pull that trigger big as life. Watched him 'tween the crack in the bathroom door. Glad he didn't have to piss! 'Been the end of old Odell Stroup.

25

Albert and Ellie rush to the window. A monster has ignited the sky: the scene outside is one of incandescent beauty with tongues of red and orange, blue and yellow leaping up up up to the heavens.

"9-1-1," shouts Bob Lesley dashing to the phone.

Paralyzed, Rose remains at the table with the others who, until three minutes ago, were enjoying cheerful if meaningless conversation and Taki's return. Everyone's thinking is identical. This is not an insignificant kitchen fire innocently started by Harriet Puffenbarger. Several crowd around the windows and watch the conflagration.

Arthur Everett stands and offers his arm to Lib.

"I hate to confess this dear, but I've been drawn to the spectacle of a fire since childhood. Let's go watch, Lib."

"Arthur! You never told me that! We don't want to get in the way, dear. Hear the sirens wailing? The trucks will be rolling by in minutes."

"Come on, Lib. Sounds as if others are going out to watch."

Excited voices escalate and muted footsteps of fellow residents hurry to the *porte-cochere*, where the Everetts quickly join them.

Ellie rushes to Rose and croaks, "It's a holocaust out there! No firecrackers, Rose. Siege, I tell you, we've under siege!"

"What else can happen, Ellie? Reed Chenowski, Jocey,

now this. Any solid suspects on your list of arsonists?"

"Oh gosh, yes, Rose," nods Ellie. "This scares the liver out of me. I was sort of thinking Bob Jenkins, because he *does* roam the halls. You know that."

"I dubbed him *'The Prowler'*, remember?"

"I do. But then Esther's stroke came and he does nothing but mope. He has the opportunity to drop the bags of stuff, but I can't pinpoint any motive. And besides, I feel sorry for him. I'm ruling Bob Jenkins out."

"Arthur just confessed to Lib that he's been fascinated by fires since he was a youngster. They've already left to watch from the steps."

"But Arthur was with *us* all evening. He didn't have the opportunity to slip out."

"Ellie, we are ignoring the obvious."

"I know. And I hate it."

"Major Featherstone. Circumstantial evidence or not, Ellie, everything we've seen and heard in the past two, three weeks points to the major's involvement."

"He's been high on my unwritten list from Day One"

"But we have no evidence, Ellie. At least I haven't. Do you?"

"Not one shred. But let's go out on the steps with the others. The distance between the steps and the cottages is great enough so we'll be in no danger. If we stay put we won't be in the way. And we just might discover what we're looking for: solid evidence."

Rose and Ellie make their way to the great hall and thread through the crowd gathering on Wynfield's broad stone steps. For the first time Rose views her aluminum walker as friend, not foe. Knots of residents part and a pathway opens as she moves to the front, Ellie tagging at her elbow.

The crackling inferno grows in magnitude. The Fincastle Fire Department arrived moments before and the firefighters are dark and shadowy specters as they struggle to contain the combustion. Looping snakes of hoses slither across the rugged terrain, pulled by unseen hands.

Shouts of "Get back! Get back!" ring out and the seniors obediently step back. A huge *boom!* and sheets of blue flame lick the velvety black of the sky.

"Fuel tank exploding. I don't like the sounds of that," Bob Lesley reports somberly.

"Is it devouring all the cottages, Bob?" Rose asks.

"Not yet. Looks to me as if the blaze started in that huge pile of brush they'd cut down for the construction. Remember the peach trees they leveled?"

"The ones you and Frances threatened to chain yourselves to in order to spare them? How could we forget?" Ellie is laughing in spite of the dire situation.

"The crew should have moved that brush weeks ago. Instead, the workmen have been tossing trash and scrap lumber on the heap and the pile has grown and grown. This fire was an accident waiting to happen."

"Peach jam."

"What's that, Rose?"

"Peach jam. Chickie told me the peach trees they cut down were the old gnarled ones, good for nothing but firewood, and when they burned, they'd smell like peach jam boiling on the stove. Sniff the air. It's peach jam, all right."

Boom! One more explosion, another gigantic spurt of blue.

"Oh, my God, another fuel tank. Peach jam and fumes. Folks are beginning to see how fearful this is. Thank God we're in a safe place, Rose." Ellie sounds worried.

"Ellie—look! Over there!" Rose is pointing to a couple on the far edge of the lawn, their identity obscured by distance and billowing smoke. The taller figure appears to be tottering, gesturing frantically.

"What were we just saying a minute ago? I think it is...yes, Major and Mrs. Featherstone, out for an evening stroll. Do you see?"

"I sure do. But what is he doing? Vinnie keeps reaching for something in Major Featherstone's hands. What's going on? I've got to get closer, Rose. It's too steep for you. Wait here. I'll try to hear what they're saying."

PEACH JAM

7 cups peaches, mashed
5 cups of sugar
Boil for 20 minutes. Stir often. Remove from heat; stir in 2 boxes of peach or apricot Jell-O.

Thelma Ribble's Favorite Recipe for Jam

CHAPTER

26

Ellie steals off to peek at the Featherstones. She is within ten feet of the couple and hears Vinnie crying, "Not fair! My turn, it's my turn!"

What is going on? The din of the fire is horrific, and Ellie strains to hear the Featherstones' words. And Vinnie! The Southern belle is frumpy and tousled, her beautiful silver hair in wild disarray. Ellie steps closer, observes Vinnie's lovely face and comprehends instantly that Vinnie has snapped, soaring like a wild bird to a secret place where nothing can reach her, not even the major.

Emboldened by these perceptions, Ellie quietly nudges Major Featherstone's arm. He is sobbing and his chest is heaving. Ellie hears nothing but dry papery rattles.

"What can I do to help you, Major?"

"Vinnie—I've lost Vinnie. She's gone back to *Belle Bois* seventy-five years back—I just can't—"

"Don't try, Major. Let her be Lavinia Whittington of the Mississippi delta. We'll get help, I promise. But I must know, Major, did Vinnie put a firecracker on the brush?"

"Five of them. Five! She'd hidden them in her gown, as well as matches from the Shenandoah Club. She wanted a stroll this evening, so I rolled her through part of the garden. Then she insisted on seeing the cottage area. It all happened so fast. I—I just don't know."

"Not fair! My turn!" Vinnie is remembering her childhood. A birthday party perhaps?

Ellie envisions the plantation with its groves of pecan trees, children in white frocks racing over the acres of green lawn that rolls to the edge of the Mississippi, servants standing quietly with silver trays of lemonade. There are mint juleps for the parents and everywhere the happy laughter of childhood and the twinkling lights of colored lanterns and fireflies in the summer nights.

"She says we must take turns lighting the sparklers."

"Major Featherstone, let me push Vinnie back up the hill. Can you manage alone if you steady yourself with your chair? Vinnie needs immediate help, and Dr. Lesley is there with Rose. He'll give Vinnie something for the night and then tomorrow we'll decide the next move. Ready? Let's go!" Ellie takes charge of this offensive.

When they reach the steps, Ellie whispers an abbreviated version of the scenario to Rose and Bob Lesley. Seeing the Featherstones are in capable hands, she scurries off to find Mrs. Gallentine.

The director is in her office, almost as disheveled as Vinnie Featherstone. She is on the phone. Ellie, still panting from her push up the hill, gratefully sinks into the nearest chair and waits.

Finally, Mrs. Gallentine hangs up and she, too, looks ready to collapse in her chair. "Have you ever seen anything like this, Mrs. Johnson? Two fires in two days?"

Ellie shakes her head and says, "I hate to add fuel to your fires, literally, but I must, Mrs. G."

"How bad can it get?" Paula's face shows the anguish of the events that are threatening to topple her reserve of steel.

"Maybe not as bad as it appears at this second. I've found our arsonist. I say 'our' because Rose and I have been tracking the same culprit that you have these past few weeks. In our case we found firecrackers she'd dropped."

Mrs. Gallentine stiffens and stares at Ellie. "Firecrackers *she* dropped? Am I hearing you, Mrs. Johnson?"

"You are. Sadly, I have to tell you that it is our Vinnie Featherstone. She has lost it. I don't know if it's a TIA or something worse, but she is not herself. I've just left Vinnie and the major with Dr. Lesley. He'll do what's best for her. And I told the major we'd cope with tomorrow when tomorrow comes."

"But...Vinnie and not the major! Why the matches? Firecrackers? A cry for attention?"

"No, I just think she has reverted to her childhood, remembering happier times with fireworks. This has probably been coming on and the major has done a good job covering for her. Until tonight. He admitted that Vinnie put the firecrackers on the pile of brush."

Paula put her head in her hands and wilts as visibly as the fading peace lily in the corner. "I'll have to turn this in, file a criminal report. Vinnie Featherstone may face serious charges."

"Maybe not," urges Ellie. "Look at it this way. The peach trees were literally dead wood, useless for anything but a good fire. They should have been hauled away weeks ago. If Bob Lesley is correct in his assessment, the construction crews are largely to blame. They've been throwing trash on that pile, plus they left fuel containers too near. If the firemen are able to confine the blaze to that one pile, none of the new construction will be damaged and the land will be cleared. What is the great loss? I don't see any."

"A good point, Mrs. Johnson."

"Ellie, please. I'm sick of this formality between us. *Paula.*"

The Resident Director laughed, relieved to feel good about something.

"Good point, *Ellie.* The fire department has been marvelous. I might be out of line, but I shall ask the construction company to make a major contribution to the fire department in lieu of my reporting their sloppiness. And if I twist it about in my head I can undoubtedly discover that a youngster may have dropped a pyrotechnical device onto that unwieldy pile of brush. It was obviously an eyesore and hazard."

"Youngster, young at heart— sounds true to me."

"And a fair solution, Mrs....Ellie. I'll go see about Mrs. Featherstone and make arrangements for—oh, before I forget, Mrs. McNess's daughter called moments before the fire started and said they were bringing Max back tomorrow. Seems they have to fly to San Francisco and want to return the dog to his mistress. If you see her before I do, Ellie, will you pass this on?"

Ellie returns to Reception and she sees that the gaggle of onlookers is dispersing. Rose, ahead of the pack, is pushing toward her. The residents straggle into the hall in two's and three's, chatting with renewed jollity and seeming reluctant for the evening's entertainment to end.

"Ellie! Good news!" Rose's eyes sparkle and her face is shiny with the light rain that is beginning to fall.

"Bob and I made our way over to the fire site and he was right. The firemen were able to contain the blaze before it reached the cottages or the new lumber. They're hosing down the embers now. And of course this rain is a blessing."

"That is blessing number one. And I have a few more to lay at your feet. Guess what Mrs. Gallentine asked me to tell you?"

"No games, Ellie, please," pleads Rose.

"Annie has just called Mrs. G. to say she and Jim have to go out of town and she is bringing Max over tomorrow. That should make your recovery complete."

"Oh, Ellie, that's the best news I've had! I know I can manage his walks now."

"We'll all help you, love. But let me tell you what Mrs. G. is going to do..."

"Find Jocey!"

"That, too, but this concerns our lovely Vinnie."

Ellie Johnson Writes It Bold And In Gold

As Rose says, 'What else can happen?' Poor Vinnie Featherstone! All of us have noticed her getting quieter these past weeks. How long has it been? Six weeks? Six weeks of quiet? Perhaps. But Major Featherstone was so noisy and talkative I think all of us assumed it was just Vinnie's nature to let him rant on and on. I wonder if that was a cover-up for his wife's mental condition? He must have known something wasn't right and didn't know how else to disguise it. Poor man! Do I feel sorrier for: Vinnie or the major? They're such a team. But medication is marvelous—look at me—cancer survivor for almost ten years. I'm living proof of what medicines can do. Oh, I hope something can help restore Vinnie's mind. She's practically a legend at Wynfield Farms. I wonder what Taki thinks about all this? Poor man, it was so quiet when he first arrived. Quite a change! Two fires, one kidnapping, one nut case. Well, I'll take care of Taki. We are simpatico—two kindred spirits. Oh God, think of all those glorious shopping trips ahead of us!

27

Charlie Caldwell is the last resident to leave the scene of the fire. Because of his volunteer hours as Chaplain in the Fincastle Fire Department he feels close to the men and women who volunteer their lives and their time. What started as part of Charlie's community service has extended into a genuine friendship with the citizens of this small town. His friends have put the fire to bed. The rain will finish the job.

He waves as the fire truck rumbles down the Wynfield driveway. Suddenly he sees coming toward him, in tandem with the departing truck, another, a small pick-up, followed by what appears to be the sheriff's car.

"Hey," he yells, "It's Jocey! Jocey is coming home to Wynfield Farms!"

So every sound tree bears good fruit,
But the bad tree bears evil fruit.
A sound tree cannot bear evil fruit,
Nor can a bad tree bear good fruit.
Every tree that does not bear good fruit is cut down
And thrown into the fire.
Thus you will know them by their fruits.
Matthew 7: 17-20 *RSV*

CHAPTER

28

"Jocey's home!" Charlie Caldwell, sedate, retired man of the cloth, becomes an irrepressible schoolboy as he skitters about shouting the news of Jocey's return. As with every resident of Wynfield Farms, Jocey Ribble is a favorite. He has prayed fervently for her safe and rapid return since news of her abduction reached his ears. The pick-up truck winding along the Wynfield driveway is a tangible sign that his prayers have been answered.

Rose is almost giddy. "Oh Ellie, do you hear Father Charlie? Let's join him to welcome Jocey. Oh, praise the Lord!"

The two friends hurry as fast as Rose's walker will allow. They reach Father Charlie's side just in time to see the familiar truck draw up and park in front of the *porte-cochere.* Jocey climbs out, stands, arms akimbo, thumbs in overalls' pockets, looking up at the welcoming party. Her dark hair is pulled back severely with a rubber band and her pale face looks taut and drawn. Dark, smudgy circles rim both her large eyes. Her shoulders sag and not surprisingly, she appears to be tired in both body and spirit. Otherwise this is the Jocey that Wynfield knows and loves.

Sheriff Hershberger struggles out of his car and joins Jocey in facing the crowd. His massive bulk easily dwarfs the pathetic girl who is now visibly wilting.

"Well folks, I told you we'd bring her back safe and

sound. Here's your gal," he booms. "Jocey, want to tell 'em in your own words?"

Jocey blushes and for the first time color floods her cheeks.

"Hey, such a welcoming party! You didn't have to call out the fire trucks!"

Everyone laughs and applauds: Jocey's return tops the evening's excitement.

"I'm fine, really. Asleep on my feet, but I'm truly fine. I want to tell everyone what happened but I've got to sit down. Could we go inside?"

Rose hugs her young friend. "Oh, Jocey, we've all been worried sick. You don't know the half of it. But come in, and tell us about this wild adventure. I'm almost afraid to ask. Is Reed Chenowski locked up?"

Jocey and the sheriff exchange guarded glances. Their eyes hold in a 'Do I tell her or do you?' duel. Sheriff Hershberger nods and says, "Go ahead, Jocey. It's your story."

Jocey slumps on the Chippendale bench by the doorway and speaks so softly that only Rose can hear, "Mrs. McNess, he's dead. Reed Chenowski is dead."

Rose gasps and shakes her head. Ellie moves closer and hugs her firmly, a genuine Ellie-kind-of-bear hug.

Rose looks at Jocey directly and asks, "Suicide, Jocey?"

An imperceptible shake of the head says 'yes'.

"I drove and drove all night. Sometimes I was helplessly lost; other times I faked it. I've never been on that part of the interstate before and that man didn't have a clue of the route to the beach. I knew I had to stall as long as possible. I didn't know what he would do after we got there. Just as I pulled onto the Virginia Beach exit I heard a siren behind us. Oh, golly, I prayed that he wouldn't hear it 'cause he was quiet then and sort of dozing. But wouldn't you know? He straightened up and poked that gun in my side and whispered, 'Get out of this fast, hear me?' Well, just then the deputy cut in front of my truck and forced me off the road. I told Chenowski that my left brake light was out—it really had been dim for a couple of days—and that was why they were stopping me. He didn't buy that, of course. Told me to do all the talking and get us out of there." Jocey stops and covers her face, shuddering at the nightmare of the past twenty-four hours.

"When the deputy stepped up to the truck both of us realized he was looking for us. His expression said it all. Chenowski yelled something like, 'I'm not going back...it's over, Rick.'"

"He was as calm as could be, just like when he shot the clerk. More than calm—icy. Like he had no emotions, no nerves. Then he jerked open the door and jumped. Ran off into the brush. It was just beginning to get light so I couldn't see. A half-second later I heard the shot. Guess I freaked out then. Something bad was bound to happen, I knew that, but I wasn't expecting this. I guess I'm still freaked out."

Sheriff Hershberger pats Jocey's shoulder affectionately. "She's a real trooper, folks. Police in Virginia Beach took excellent care of her a good part of the day. Debriefing, details of the shooting, all that business. They'll remember Miss Jocelyn Ribble of Fincastle for a long, long time."

"How about her parents Sheriff?"

"Yes, Sheriff, have the Ribbles been notified?"

"Sure have. First thing after we made sure Miss Ribble was safe and unharmed. Sent one of my men over to tell 'em personally. About four o'clock I guess it was."

"And I guess if they tried to call us we were busy with supper and then the fire..." says Ellie.

"Deputy said Chenowski died instantly. Put the bullet through his heart, clean as the old whistle. Body will be brought back here to Roanoke for I.D. and an autopsy. I feel right bad for you Miz McNess. Old friend of yours, wasn't he?"

Ellie had brought a chair for Rose as Jocey began her narration. Rose takes a long and deep breath before responding to the Sheriff.

"Old friend from old days, Sheriff, too far in the past for my mind to comprehend fully even now. I feel so bad for you, Jocey. How could he put you through all of this? Reed must have been desperate. In every sense of the word. Finally his guilt and doubts and demons must have tortured him to self-destruction. Somehow his suicide does not surprise me. He couldn't face what he knew was waiting on him—a trial for attempted murder, kidnapping charges and who knows what else. He took the coward's way out—again. I'm sad and relieved. Mostly relieved, and that is the truth. But how are you, Jocey, really? Tell me Mr. Chenowski didn't harm you."

"He didn't, Mrs. McNess. Scared me purple, but harm me? No. I think he came to respect me. He wasn't really evil, at least I don't think so. Except when he shot the guy at the Mobil station."

"Who is doing well, incidentally," breaks in Sheriff Hershberger. "He really pulled your chestnut out of the fire, Jocey. Him and a character named Odell Stroup. Seems Stroup picked up a hitchhiker one day in Daleville, fellow needing a ride to Wynfield Farms. Stroup's a canny old bird, farmer over on the James. Noticed that snake tattoo on Chenowski's wrist. Old Stroup stopped for gas last night at the same Mobil station, just before you drove in, and had enough sense to stay put in the gent's. He got a glimpse of Chenowski before he shut the door. Identified him from the description we gave him. Yep, 'Stroup sounds like soup' helped save you, Jocey. The Chenowski guy was savvy enough to let *you* pick up the can of oil, but he pulled the trigger."

"Yipes!" pipes Jocey, eyes widening at the thought. "I never guessed that. Was *I* your shooting suspect?"

"You were never under *our* suspicion, Jocey," Ellie says with intensity. "But tell me, child, he didn't, uh, take advantage of you in any way, did he?"

"Oh, Ellie," Rose says with a sigh. "You put that so delicately. Where I hesitate you plunge in fearlessly."

Jocey shakes her head adamantly. "Absolutely not. I was beginning to tell you, when he shot the clerk, that's the only time I really got nervous and awfully scared. The rest of the time he made me drive and listen to him talk. Talk, talk, talk. I heard his life story over and over again. But I was in control. And I happened to have *this* in my overalls. I was ready to gouge him like a dandelion if he tried anything." She reaches into her overalls and produces a heavy metal gardening tool with a forked point.

Laughter fills the air—the nervous laughter of people relieved to laugh again.

"Mrs. McNess, Reed Chenowski asked me to make sure you got this. He really, really liked you, you know." Jocey pulls a folded newspaper clipping from her back pocket.

Rose takes the piece of paper, wrinkled and torn at the corners where it has been folded. She spreads it over her knees and smoothes it as best she can. From *The Roanoke Times,* dated March 10, 2003, the article is a plea for lifeguards from the '60's to contact Virginia Beach for immediate summer employment.

Again Rose shakes her head in disbelief. "I guess he saved this to prove to the world that he was coming back to Virginia to lifeguard one more time. His ticket of admission." She crumples the paper and shoves it into her pocket.

"Gosh, do you think I can go on home now, Sheriff Hershberger? Suddenly my legs are turning to Jell-O."

"May I drive you home, Jocey?" No one has noticed Chef Leon joining the circle of listeners. He is standing off to one side, quietly absorbing Jocey's every word.

Jocey and Chef Leon look at each other and walk noiselessly from the Reception Hall.

Rose and Paula stand together on the Wynfield steps and watch the two vehicles drive away, Chef Leon taking Jocey home to her anxious family and Sheriff Hershberger to headquarters to wind up details of 'that lifeguard case'.

When the winking red taillights are no longer visible, Rose breaks the silence. "Change is constant."

"Pardon?" asks Mrs. Gallentine.

"Forgive me, Mrs. Gallentine-rhymes-with-valentine. I'm just muttering. Quoting something that Arthur Everett is always saying: 'Change is constant.' Sounds better in Latin, something like *'mutatio est constans.'* Of course I'm not the Latin scholar Arthur is, but the meaning is the same."

"I agree. True words no matter what the language. Our Jocey is back, thank the good Lord. Mr. Chenowski won't bother you again. The firecracker episode is behind us, and Taki has come to stay. Talk about constant change!"

"Will you speak to the Board about Taki's so-called residency?"

"I don't have to, but I shall. I'm convinced they'll look forward to it. He's a quiet, self-effacing man. How could they do other *than* approve his extended stay?"

"Ummm. 'Extended stay.' I like that. That's also a reassuring phrase for Mr. Chenowski's fate. Sad, how little peace he found in his lifetime." Rose takes a long breath. "You know, suddenly I am exhausted. All of the day's excitement has gotten to me."

"I don't doubt it. I'm feeling washed out myself, and I don't have a hangnail much less a new hip. Whoops! I almost forgot. This FAX came for you as I was leaving the office."

"A FAX? Let's see. Oh, from David Heath-Nesbit, my English guide. He's coming to Wynfield Farms! The grandchild's mysterious illness has cleared up and he's packing to come for a visit." Rose chuckles. "And don't worry, David's *not* a lifeguard!"

"What was it you were saying about change? This evening closes an eventful chapter in your life, Rose McNess, and another one begins. I'm happy for you. You're a strong and classy lady. Wynfield Farms is fortunate to have you here."

"Oh no, Mrs. Gallentine, I'm the fortunate one in having Wynfield Farms. Unlike lifeguards, my friends here are true safeguards."

Postscript

ROSE MCNESS still lives happily at Wynfield Farms when she isn't traveling the world. Her close friend DAVID HEATH-NESBITT visits annually, usually in the spring, when he and Rose take many walks and short trips together. They have escorted two groups of residents to Italy on separate occasions and are currently planning to explore Eastern Europe next year.

MAX, Rose's beloved Scottish terrier, is arthritic but moderately active and remains at his mistress's side from morning to night, whenever his mistress is in residence.

PROFESSOR YOKAMURA returned to his native Japan after completing one year as "Visiting Scholar."

ELLIE JOHNSON accompanied the professor as his secretary and has not yet returned to Wynfield Farms.

Discovering to her delight that all of Australia is a laboratory for lichenologists, FRANCES KEYNES-LIVINGSTON leased her apartment at Wynfield Farms, moved to Melbourne, and married, not Dr. Evan Wickham-Biggs but his young and brilliant Field Assistant, Dr. Winslow Nebaard.

JOCELYN RIBBLE and CHEF LEON married shortly after what the community refers to as "that kidnapping episode." They are expecting their first child in six months.

Extensive neurological tests revealed that VINNIE FEATHERSTONE was suffering from an inoperable brain tumor; she died less than three weeks after starting the fire at Wynfield Farms, as exquisite as ever until her final days.

MAJOR FEATHERSTONE resumed his solitary walks and has been seen squiring a new resident (a widow from Richmond) with some frequency.

On those rare occasions when REED CHENOWSKI's name is mentioned in Rose McNess' presence, the lady merely shakes her head and remarks, "As happy and content as I am here in my castle, it is hard to imagine what a sad, nomadic life that poor man endured."

Indeed...

Photo by King Photography

BARBARA DICKINSON'S previous novels, the critically acclaimed *A Rebellious House* and *Small House, Large World*, reflect both her love for the state of Virginia and comprehension of the complexities of aging. In this, her third in the Wynfield Farms trilogy, she examines what happens when her characters encounter visitors from the past. Mysterious happenings abound!

Barbara is a graduate of Wellesley College and received a Master of Arts in Liberal Studies from Hollins University.

A frequent contributor to the Book Page of the *Roanoke Times*, she is also a columnist for a local seniors' magazine.

When not traveling, Barbara Dickinson lives in Roanoke with her husband Billy, and her Scottish terrier Maxine.

OTHER BOOKS BY
BARBARA M. DICKINSON

_____ *A Rebellious House* $ _____
QTY   1-55618-185-X $10.00

_____ *Small House, Large World* $_____
QTY   1-55618-182-5 $10.00

_____ *Lifeguards...and Safeguards* $_____
QTY   0-9747278-0-6 $10.00

      VA RESIDENTS ADD *4.5%* SALES TAX $_____

Shipping: $3.00 first copy; $.50 each additional $_____

     TOTAL $_____

- -

Please send me the books I have checked above. I am enclosing $ _____ .
Send check or money order, no cash or C.O.Ds please.

Inscription? Personalization upon request. Otherwise, books will be signed by author.

Name:_____   Phone:_____
Address: _____
City/State/Zip:_____

Please make your check payable to: Barbara M. Dickinson

Mail or FAX to:

Barbara M. Dickinson
2616 Stanley Avenue, SE
Roanoke, VA 24014-5042
FAX: (540) 343-8959
Phone: (540) 345-5042

Rose...and Max...and Barbara Dickinson sincerely thank you for your order!